A STREET DOG
NAMED
Pup

GILL LEWIS

David Fickling Books

31 Beaumont Street
Oxford OX1 2NP, UK

A Street Dog Named Pup
is a
DAVID FICKLING BOOK

First published in Great Britain in 2021 by
David Fickling Books,
31 Beaumont Street,
Oxford, OX1 2NP

www.davidficklingbooks.com

Hardback edition published 2021
This edition published 2022

Text and illustrations © Gill Lewis

Cover art by Levi Pinfold

978-1-78845-220-5

1 3 5 7 9 10 8 6 4 2

Papers used by David Fickling Books are from
well-managed forests and other responsible sources.

DAVID FICKLING BOOKS Reg. No. 8340307

A CIP catalogue record for this book is available from the British Library.

Typeset in Sabon by Falcon Oast Graphic Art Ltd.

Printed and bound in Great Britain by Clays Ltd, Elcograf S.p.A.

For
Roger, for his kindness and compassion
to all the animals in his care
and for
Georgie, Beth and Jemma, who are my world,
and for
Liz Cross, who met Pup first

In memory of Murphy
'*Starlake Sirius*'

When a dog gives you its love, it is a gift.
A gift to be treasured with all your heart and soul.

PUP

BREED: GERMAN SHEPHERD
/BELGIAN MALINOIS CROSS

A dog with a big heart.
He will follow you to
the ends of the earth.

Will howl when lonely.

FRENCHI

BREED: FRENCH BULLDOG

A true friend. Will help
anyone in need.

Being a short-nosed breed,
he can find it hard
to breathe.

REX

BREED: PIT BULL TERRIER CROSS

Soft and gentle soul.
However, he will fiercely
defend those he loves.

Very mistrustful
of strangers.

SAFFY

BREED: LABRADOR

Kind and gentle.
Always ready to give hugs.

Sometimes others will
take advantage of her
trusting nature.

LADY FIFI

BREED: JACK RUSSELL/
SHIH TZU CROSS

A small dog with a
big attitude.

Will bite unless regularly
pampered.

CLOWN

BREED: BOXER

Full of life and fun.

Mischief and mayhem
follow him wherever
he goes.

REYNARD

BREED: FOXHOUND

A gentle, sensitive soul.
He will happily sit for
cuddles all day.

Scared of loud noises,
he often seeks quiet and
dark places for comfort.

MERLE

BREED: BORDER COLLIE

Highly intelligent and active.

She can become bored
and anxious if unable
to work.

Prologue
THE GREAT SKY WOLF

There is a story that every mother dog will pass to her new-born pups. She will tell it to them before their eyes have opened, when they are still blind and squirming at her belly, searching for her milk. She will tell it to them when their warm plump bodies are snuggled together in sleep. She will tell it, even though her heart breaks and breaks by telling it, for she has only a short precious time when she can truly call them her own. For it is every mother's grief that she will lose her pups to man.

She will curl her body around her pups and lick each of them in turn. 'Hush now,' she'll say, 'for the stars are bright tonight and the Great Sky Wolf is running fleet-footed across the night. We must run with him, back to the time when dogs formed their bond with man. You must know this story, my little children, and hold it deep inside. For this bond was forged in the stars, when ice and fire shaped this world. In your lifetime, man may falter and forget this bond between you, and so it will be up to you to remember, and let it for ever be your guide.'

The pups will whimper, squirm closer to each other and then settle as she begins the story.

'In the time before time,' she'll say, 'there were great forests and fast rivers that roared down from the mountains. It was a time when man and wolf were equal and when the gods Orion – the great hunter – and Lupus – the great wolf – roamed the skies. Man and wolf spoke with the same tongue. They lived the same lifespan, a year for a year. But they were wary of each other for they shared the same landscape and hunted the same game. For many years, there was plenty for all and so wolf and man would bow their heads in greeting to each other but keep their distance. Wolf and man had different skills. Wolf was fast-footed, fierce and brave. Man was an inventor, and he learned to be the master of fire.

'But a great creeping cold came over the land. Ice formed where rivers had once flowed. And as the deer moved south, the wolves and men moved south with them. But the cold followed, freezing the ground as hard as rock, and soon there was little left to hunt. Both wolf and man grew hungry and began to fight each other for what was left. The sky gods, Orion and Lupus, called a truce and said that their people could share their skills to survive. And so wolves and man came to live with each other. They hunted together. They shared their lives together. They grew old together. And in return for a place by the fire, the wolves protected men from the wild creatures of the night.

'Now it came to pass that the great ice rivers retreated to the mountains and the deer returned to the valleys. Many of the wolves slipped away into the forests to live as packs once more. But one wolf, Sirius, and his family chose to stay with man. And on a cold crystal night, beneath a winter moon, Lupus came down to Earth to speak with him.

'"Sirius," said the Great Sky Wolf. "It is time to return to the mountains and end your partnership with man."

'"I cannot," said Sirius, "for I love his children as I love my own."

'Lupus growled thunder across the land. "This is not the way of the wolf. If you do not leave him, I shall take away your language, so you can neither speak words with man, nor howl with wolves. You shall be known as Dog, a servant of man."

'Sirius closed his eyes. "I cannot leave him, for he needs me more than he will ever know."

'Lupus cast his words and Sirius could now only speak in yelps and barks. Yet it made no difference, because man and dog still understood each other without the need for words.

3

'"You are a dumb animal in the eyes of man," said Lupus. "I will give you one more chance to become wolf again."

'Sirius bowed his head to Lupus. "It is my wish to protect man and his family. We love each other as equals. We live together and grow old together."

'Lupus was greatly angered. "You betray wolfkind. I will not allow it. If you do not leave man, I will cut short your life, and you shall age seven years to his one. You shall grow old, while your human does not."

'Sirius bent his head in grief, because he knew what was to come. "I cannot leave man, for I love him more than life itself."

'"Then so be it," thundered Lupus, and in his rage his words shot like lightning from his mouth.

'Man woke to find Sirius old, grey-muzzled and dead at his feet, and man grieved for his lost brother and the years they could never have. He held Sirius in his arms and wept. "I will protect your family, now and for always," he vowed, "for you truly are the greatest friend to man."

'When Lupus saw what he had done, he howled for all the world to hear, because it was only then he understood the great bond of love and trust between man and dog. He gathered the soul of Sirius between his paws. "My friend," he said to Sirius. "Your children may give their heart to man in their lifetime. But I ask them not to turn away from their wolf-brothers, for they share the same wild soul. I ask that when their time on Earth has ended, they give their soul back to me."

'"We will," said Sirius. "Now and for always."

'The Great Wolf lifted Sirius up into the skies and set him next to Orion as a sign of loyalty for all to see. And now the brightest star in the sky shines from the great dog's heart. It is a reminder of that bond between man and dog. It is a bond of faith that must never be broken.'

And the mother dog will finish her story and gently pull her puppies closer, knowing she can only protect them for this short time. She will tell them that even if man forgets the vow he made, they must always keep their faith. In times of trouble, when they are lost or frightened, they must look to the brightest star and remember this story, because the sacred bond made between man and dog is the only thing that will keep them safe.

Then her heart will break and break and break again. For she cannot know if it will be kind and gentle hands that first hold her beloved pups.

She cannot know what lies ahead for each of them, when they are taken from her, into the world of man.

Chapter 1
DEAD DOG ALLEY

Pup curled up in the footwell of the car. He tucked his nose into his fur and shivered. Nothing felt right. Freezing air blasted from a vent beside him, bringing the smells of cars, burger bars and wet tarmac. Street lights flashed by as the big man steered through the city. The windscreen wipers clunked from side to side against the heavy rain. Pup shivered again, but it wasn't from the cold. Worry chewed at him. Something was different. The car was the same. Pup usually sat on the boy's lap in the back seat. *His* boy, who smelled deliciously of football socks and cheese puffs. *His* boy, who held him tight and told him that one day he would grow into his big puppy paws and be the *biggest dog ever*. *His* boy, who he tumbled with across the park in warm sunshine, pushing the football with his nose, while his boy ran after him laughing and shouting.

But his boy wasn't here this time.

It was dark and cold.

'Good dog,' said the big man.

Pup wagged the tip of his tail, but this didn't feel right. Other dogs were easy to understand, but the language of the humans was confusing. What they said with their body was often different from the words they used. Nothing else about the big man said *good dog*. The big man was silent and closed. His hands were on the steering wheel, staring ahead. Pup couldn't read him at all.

Pup wanted to whine and yip, but he worried the big man

would shout at him and slap him across the nose. He always did when Pup made a noise.

If his boy had been in the car, Pup would have crawled up into his lap and tucked his head onto his chest and listened to the thump, thump, thump of his boy's heart. His boy would have scratched just behind his ears and held him safe.

But his boy wasn't here this time.

His boy was still at home, in bed where Pup should be with him now. In his mind he could still see his boy in bed and himself curled up beside him. The boy always wrapped his arm around Pup, holding Pup's paw in his warm human hand. They would lie curled up beneath the fleecy blanket, while the boy fell asleep, breathing warm breath into Pup's soft fur. But this night had been different too. The boy's mother had come in. She had lifted Pup up, placing a teddy beside the boy where Pup had been.

Good dog, she'd said, while she placed the sleeping boy's arm over the teddy instead.

We're going for a walk, she'd whispered to Pup. But there had been no lead, or ball. Only the big man waiting at the door to put Pup inside the car.

Pup tucked his nose deeper into his fur as the car lurched and swung along the roads. He could still smell his boy in his fur, and there felt some safety in that.

Pup fell into an uncomfortable sleep, jolting and sliding on the rubber mat.

When he woke, the car had stopped in a dark street. The big man got out and lit a cigarette.

Pup climbed onto the seat and peered out. This wasn't

9

the park. It didn't smell like the park. It didn't smell like anywhere he'd been before. The road was lit by a single lamppost at the far end. A halo of rain-fizzled light circled the lamp. There were no houses, just an old garage, boarded-up shops and an empty car park. Pup felt himself lifted up from the car seat and taken outside.

The big man slipped off Pup's collar.

Pup felt strange without his collar, naked and unowned.

'Be quick,' the big man said.

This was the command to go to the toilet. The big man would praise him if he went outside. Pup wanted to please him, so he trotted to a wall and lifted his leg. There were the scents of other dogs on the wall, and Pup wondered who they were. A shiver ran through him.

The car door slammed.

Pup spun around to look, but the man was already inside the car. 'Uff!' called Pup.

Had the big man forgotten him?

'Uff!' Pup ran towards the car, but it started up in a belch of exhaust smoke and sped away, spraying dirty water in Pup's face. Pup ran after it. He ran and ran, but his big puppy paws tripped over each other and he tumbled and slid face first into an oily puddle.

'Uff!' barked Pup. He scrambled to his feet and began running again but couldn't keep up. 'Uff, uff, uff! Wait for me. Wait for me. Wait for me.'

Pup's heart thumped inside his chest. The big man had forgotten him. Surely he'd realize Pup wasn't in the car and come back for him?

The car turned the corner, leaving Pup in the darkness. He stopped and stared at the place where the car had once been.

A cold wind funnelled down the street, blowing loose paper into the sky. Rain soaked deep into his fur.

Pup looked up and down the empty street.

There was no one.

Nothing looked or smelled familiar.

Dark alleyways led off from the road.

He tucked his tail between his legs.

The wind whistled through the telephone wires and rattled the tin roof of the garage.

Further down the street, a metal bin lid clanged to the floor and rolled out from an alleyway.

There was a cough too. Someone was there. Pup wondered if it might be someone who could help him. He kept close to the wall and edged down the street until he stopped at the alleyway.

Something was in there. Pup could hear a snorting and snuffling in the shadows. It was coming closer and closer and smelled of another dog. It might be one of the scary big dogs at the park – his boy used to lift him up into his arms and protect him from them.

But his boy wasn't here.

Pup whined, tucked his tail further between his legs and backed away.

A deep rasping voice spoke out from the darkness.

'Welcome,' it said, 'to Dead Dog Alley.'

Chapter 2
FRENCHI

THE DOG THAT EMERGED FROM the shadows was much smaller than Pup had guessed. He was smaller than Pup. Or at least he was shorter. He had a barrel-shaped body, short bandy legs and a stubby tail. His ears were large and rounded and he had a face so squashed that he looked like he had run full speed into a brick wall. He was all white, except for a large patch of black over his right eye. He snuffled and snorted through his nose, and when he breathed his wide tongue hung so far out he looked like he was gulping air.

The dog circled around him. 'A pup, eh? A big one, though. How old are you?'

Pup just stared at the dog. The dog's ears were pricked and his stubby tail upright. He didn't look fierce, but he didn't look like he wanted to play either.

The dog continued walking around him, inspecting him. 'Hmm, huge puppy paws, but starting to get long lanky legs. A bit skinny too. Six months old, are you? Not looking so cute any more, I suspect.' He pushed his face nearer to Pup. 'What was it? Chewing everything? Yelping all day?'

Pup backed away and found himself pressed up against the wall. He blinked hard in confusion. 'What was what?' he said.

'Why did they dump you?' asked the dog. 'Why did your humans dump you?'

'They haven't dumped me,' Pup said.

'So what are you doing here?' said the dog.

Pup glanced back up the street, hoping to see the head-lights of the big man's car. 'The big man forgot to pick me up,' he said.

The dog tipped his head on one side. 'Forgot?'

'Yes,' whimpered Pup. But now he wasn't so sure. His thoughts felt all tangled up and he kept thinking about his boy still in bed, where he should be now. 'He'll come back.'

The dog sat down and attempted to scratch his ear with his back foot, but couldn't quite reach, so he rubbed his ear on the corner of the wall instead. 'That's what they always say. But we all get dumped here, sooner or later. That's why it's called Dead Dog Alley.'

Pup whined and tucked his tail between his legs.

'What's your name?' asked the dog.

'I'm Pup,' said Pup.

'I know you're a pup,' said the dog, 'I can see that. What's your name? What was the first name you were given?'

'It's just Pup,' said Pup again. 'That's my name.'

'Well that's a daft name for a pup like you, if you ask me,' said the dog. 'You won't be a pup for ever and you're going to be huge.' He peered a little closer. 'I reckon you're a barker. Did you bark much?'

'Sometimes,' said Pup. 'Only when they left me. But they always heard me, because if I kept barking they came back in the end.'

'I expect your barking brought the neighbours around too,' said the dog.

'How did you know?' asked Pup.

'And,' said the dog, 'I'm guessing you think you're an

15

excellent guard dog. Every day, the same person would arrive at the house, shove paper and packages through a hole in the front door and then go away.'

Pup curled his lips to show his line of pointy teeth. 'That's right. Every time they came, I barked and barked at them, and they never dared come in. I scared them off each time. They just left packages and went.'

'And you ripped up the packages and pieces of paper?' said the dog.

'Ripped them to shreds,' Pup said proudly.

The dog sighed. 'Your humans dumped you, Pup. You might as well hear it from me. Humans don't like chewers or barkers. They don't want you any more.'

'My boy wants me,' said Pup. 'My boy will find me.'

The dog licked at a red sore on his left front paw. 'So there's a boy, is there? How old?'

Pup felt the worry chew at him again. 'I don't know.'

'How big is he?' said the dog.

'He came up to the big man's shoulders,' said Pup.

The dog sighed and shook his head. 'Well, I reckon he's about ten human years. Old enough to miss you. And that's hard,' he said.

'What's hard?' said Pup.

'Even if your boy wants to find you, he won't know where to look,' said the dog.

Pup felt the worry knot inside him. It was the same worry he felt every time the humans left him in the house on his own. But here he was in a place he didn't know, with a dog he didn't know.

The dog sighed. 'You may as well follow me and get out of this rain,' he said. 'My name's Frenchi, by the way.'

Pup just stared after the dog.

Frenchi started walking away. 'Well, are you coming?'

Pup looked up and down the road. It was bleak and empty. He sat down and whined.

Frenchi turned. 'I expect you're wondering if you can trust me?'

Pup whined again. He didn't know this dog. He just wanted his boy.

Frenchi shook the rain from his coat and took a step towards Pup. 'Look, it's a hard lesson to learn, but you can't trust anyone, not any more. You're on your own. You have to trust your instincts now.'

'I'm staying here,' said Pup. 'My boy will find me. He always does. My boy will come.' The worry bubbled up inside him and came out as a howl, a long howl rising into the night.

'Blimey!' said Frenchi. 'A howler. And that's an impressive howl. No wonder they dumped you.'

Pup took another deep breath and howled again, a cry from his heart calling out across the city. Calling out to his boy.

'Well,' said Frenchi. 'Can't hang about. With all that noise, the Snatchers will be here soon.'

Pup stopped mid-howl. 'The Snatchers?'

Frenchi shuddered and backed into the shadows. 'You don't want the Snatchers to find you.'

'Who are the Snatchers?' asked Pup.

But Frenchi was already trotting away into the darkness of the alleyway, huffing and snuffling as he went.

Pup stared after him, then turned back to the road. He would wait. The rain seemed to come down even harder, soaking deep through his fur. He shivered and hunched his back against the wind. He was good at waiting. Sometimes at home he had to wait for hours for his boy.

Sure enough, headlights swung into the road, filling the darkness with beams of light. Pup wagged his tail. Frenchi had been wrong. Pup knew the big man would return. He sat up straight, paws together and waited for the big man to find him. Maybe his boy would be in the car too, and Pup would be ready to leap into his boy's arms and lick his face while his boy held him tightly. Pup's legs felt like coiled springs. He couldn't stop himself – he jumped up and bounded towards the car.

But then he stopped, his paws sliding on the wet pavement.

This car didn't sound like the big man's car. It was bigger too. It was a van that stopped a little way down the road. Two humans climbed out. The smell of them drifted down towards Pup and he didn't recognize them. They smelled of many things, of humans and other dogs and bleached floors. They smelled of lots of dogs all mixed up together. One human carried a long pole with a rope, while the other carried a torch, swinging the beam from side to side, scanning the street.

Fear rose up inside Pup. His paws felt stuck to the tarmac. The beam of the torch swung closer and closer to him. Soon it would reach him.

This didn't feel right.

It didn't feel right at all.

He had to make a choice, between a dog he'd never met before and two humans approaching with a rope and pole.

Trust your instincts, the dog had said.

Pup took a deep breath and slipped into the shadows. 'Wait, Frenchi,' he called. 'Wait for me.'

Chapter 3
THE RAILWAY DEN

PUP CAUGHT UP WITH FRENCHI and trotted alongside him in the alleyway.

'Where are we going?' asked Pup.

'To meet the boss,' said Frenchi.

'The boss?'

'Come on,' said Frenchi. 'We'll talk later. Let's get out of this rain.'

Frenchi stopped at the far end of the alleyway and looked out. The next street was wide and well lit. It was busy with traffic. Cars and lorries raced by in both directions, spraying water into the air. A cyclist whizzed past them on the pavement.

Frenchi turned to look at Pup. 'I'm guessing you don't know much about cars.'

'Park,' said Pup, saying the first thing that came into his head. 'Cars take you to the park.'

Frenchi shook his head. 'Here they'll kill you. They won't see you and you'll be under the wheels and squashed flat before you know it.'

Pup watched the cars rushing past.

'You have to wait for the gaps between,' said Frenchi. 'Stay close to me.'

Frenchi shuffled to the edge of the pavement. The headlights seemed like a river of light. But then the cars stopped in a line further down the road.

'Now!' said Frenchi, shuffling across. 'The cars stop at those lights. We haven't got long. Come on, hurry.'

Pup followed. The traffic started up again and a lorry rumbled towards them. Pup turned to see it bearing down on him. The monster's headlights caught him and pinned him to the ground. He couldn't run, he couldn't move. He crouched lower and lower as the lorry rose above him.

'Move!' shouted Frenchi.

But Pup couldn't move.

The lorry shuddered to a stop, with a hiss and puff of air brakes. It blasted its horn and the sound filled Pup's body and deafened him. In the kaleidoscope of car lights, street lights and bright white needles of rain, he could see Frenchi coming towards him, and feel him shoving his nose behind him and pushing him across to the pavement. The lorry man was yelling at them, but Frenchi kept pushing Pup down another alleyway. He stopped when they were in the shadows.

'That was close,' panted Frenchi. He sat down to catch his breath. 'Oh boy, you've got a lot to learn.'

Pup sank down beside him and licked his paws. They felt sore where the grit from the road had worked their way in between his pads. The cold rain soaked through to his skin and his whole body ached. He curled up, tucking his nose into his fur.

'We can't stop,' said Frenchi gently. 'It's not far now.'

But Pup screwed his eyes shut, hoping everything would disappear. He wanted to open them and be back with his boy.

Frenchi tried to push him again, but Pup curled up even more tightly and refused to move.

'For the love of Lupus,' swore Frenchi, 'we can't stay out here. We'll freeze to death.'

But Pup wouldn't listen.

Frenchi bent down and closed his teeth on Pup's tail, giving it a sharp nip. Pup yelped and jumped to his feet.

'Sorry about that,' said Frenchi. 'We can't stop.' He pressed his nose against Pup and pushed him on again, deeper into the heart of the city.

The buildings grew up tall around them and towered high into the air, showing only a strip of night sky tinged orange from the city lights. Frenchi led the way, keeping in the shadows, passing shops and offices. He turned down another street that ran along the back of a railway station. A few taxis were lined up, the drivers warm in their cabs and wishing for their night shifts to be over. They didn't notice the two dogs that trotted past them in the rain. Then Frenchi turned sharply into a gap in a wall and led the way down some steep steps that were green and slippery. Pup wrinkled his nose. It smelled damp and mouldy, and of human toilets. The bottom of the steps opened out onto a dark road that ran alongside the arches beneath a railway bridge. A train rumbled overhead, its bright windows briefly illuminating the street. In the fleeting strobes of light, Pup could see rainwater gushing along the gutters, and pooling where plastic bags and polystyrene cups clogged and jostled in the drains. The railway arches were used as stores and garages. Some had steel shutters and others were boarded up. Graffiti had been scribbled on the walls, and bins overflowed with rubbish.

Frenchi stopped at one of the archways where a bush seemed to grow out of the wall itself. 'In here,' he said. He slipped behind the bush and pushed against a loose panel of wood. Pup followed, sliding through into a dark space on the other side.

'This is the Railway Den,' said Frenchi. 'This is home. You'd better meet the boss.'

It was dry inside and out of the wind and rain. The air was stale and smelled of wet dogs. A dull glow from a white light on the back wall lit up a jumble of discarded rubbish. There was the burned-out shell of a car, and a mountain of boxes and black plastic bags with an old mattress precariously placed on top.

A deep growl came from one of the shadows and a huge black dog rose to its feet. It was bigger than any dog Pup had ever seen, with broad shoulders and a massive head. It walked out of the darkness, its eyes fixed on Pup.

Frenchi lowered his head. 'It's only me – Frenchi. And a friend.'

The dog walked closer. Even in the dim light, Pup could see its hackles were risen. It curled its lip and its teeth caught the light and gleamed. It pushed its nose towards Pup and sniffed. Pup tucked his tail between his legs and sank to the floor, trying to make himself as small as possible. His whole body trembled. Even the shadows couldn't hide this dog's presence. It was as if this dog had been formed from the darkness itself.

Frenchi tried to place himself between the dog and Pup. 'Don't scare him, Rex. This is Pup. He's lost, like us. His humans dumped him. I found him in Dead Dog Alley.'

The big dog stared at Frenchi for a moment, then turned and silently slipped back into the shadows, but Pup had the feeling he was still watching his every move.

'Is that the boss?' whispered Pup.

'No, that's Rex,' said Frenchi. 'He's OK. You've got to give him some space. Don't crowd him, remember that.'

Pup shivered. If that wasn't the boss, he didn't want to find out who was.

'Come on,' urged Frenchi. 'The boss will be expecting us now.'

In the dim light, Pup could make out several dog shapes in the gloom. They were lying on sacking and newspapers spread out across the floor. A slim Border collie slipped through the shadows. She trotted a wide arc around the pile of rubbish with the mattress, circling the dogs until she reached Pup.

'One, two, three, four, five and me . . .' she counted. She stopped in front of Pup, her head lowered, and her gaze fixed on him. 'One more,' she said. 'One more.'

Pup could see she had one eye the colour of night and one eye the colour of a summer sky. Her stare was so intense that he had to look away. He looked around, trying to see the other dogs hidden in the shadows.

'Hello, Merle,' said Frenchi. 'This is Pup. He needs a place to stay.'

Merle sniffed at him. 'One more.' She circled him once, then lay back down in her resting place, still watching Pup, her ears pricked and her blue eye reflecting the light.

A yellow Labrador shuffled forward. She had a greying muzzle, and the deepest darkest eyes Pup had seen in any dog. 'Looking for lost souls again, Frenchi? Will you never learn?'

'Hello, Saffy,' said Frenchi.

Saffy sniffed at Pup. 'Just a puppy,' she sighed. 'Too young. Much too young.'

There was something about this dog that made Pup feel warm and safe. Something deep inside him held a memory of a dog like Saffy. He wanted her to wash his face and ears. He wanted to curl up against her and fall asleep beside her.

He whined and took a step closer, but before he could reach her, a tall foxhound pushed himself between them.

The foxhound's whole body trembled, his ears alert and his nose sniffing for danger. 'Are the horsemen here, Saffy? I hear them!'

'It's just the wind, Reynard,' said Saffy, licking his face as a mother might lick a new-born pup. 'Go back to sleep.'

Reynard tucked his long tail between his legs and spun around to look at the loose boards banging in the wind. 'Don't let the Huntsman in. Don't let him in.'

'The Huntsman?' whispered Pup.

Reynard turned his gaze to Pup, and Pup could see one side of the foxhound's face was disfigured and caved in. There was no eye where an eye should have been; instead the crumpled eye socket and jaw were criss-crossed with scars.

Reynard didn't take his good eye from Pup. 'Did you see the Huntsman?'

'This is Pup,' said Saffy. 'He's a friend.'

'There are bluebells in the spring,' said Reynard. 'They sing to the trees. Have you heard them?'

Pup backed away.

'He'll take your eye,' said Reynard. 'He took mine. Follow the night prowlers. They'll keep us safe. The night prowlers know everything.'

'You're safe, Reynard,' said Saffy, pushing him away from Pup. 'Sleep now. You're safe with us.'

Pup wanted to stay close to Saffy, but Reynard stood in his way, looking through him, as if there were things Pup couldn't see.

'The Huntsman rides an iron mare,' whimpered Reynard, fixing his eye on the entrance to the den. 'He's coming. I hear him coming.'

A loud bang came from the entrance to the den, and Pup spun around to see a dark shadow moving at speed towards him. Before Pup had a chance to jump away, it knocked him off his feet and whirled around him.

'Clown,' called Merle. 'Slow down.'

Pup picked himself up to see a large boxer dog pounce down in front of him, his long tail whipping side to side.

'Who's this?' wuffed the dog, spinning away again. His long tail caught Pup across the face.

Pup turned around, trying to see where this dog would jump at him again.

'This is Pup,' said Merle. She circled the dogs again, counting after Clown's arrival. 'One, two, three, four, five, six, one more and me. Seven of us now, and me. All here,' she said. 'All here.'

Clown bounced around Pup, his paws skittering on the concrete floor.

Pup pressed himself to the ground again, trying to avoid Clown, but Clown stopped and pushed his face against Pup's.

'Hello, Pup,' barked Clown.

'For the love of Lupus,' snapped Frenchi, 'calm down, Clown. Give the pup some space.'

Pup just stared at Clown. Maybe if he'd met this dog in the park with his boy, he'd want to play, but he didn't know the rules here.

'What's he doing here?' asked Clown, sniffing Pup all over.

'He's here to meet the boss,' said Frenchi.

A trilling growl came from the mattress teetering high on the piles of rubbish.

All the dogs turned to look.

Frenchi lowered his head. 'Pup, meet our pack leader.'

The light threw long shadows against the curved brick-work of the archway, and the giant shadow of a dog's head loomed up on the far wall.

Chapter 4
MALINOIS MONGREL

THE SHADOW ON THE FAR wall grew bigger and bigger, until the dog with the trilling growl put her head over the top of the mattress. She wasn't the huge dog Pup was expecting from the size of the shadow. Instead, a tiny terrier stared down at him. She was perched on the top of the mattress, next to an open handbag.

'Fifi,' said Frenchi. 'This is Pup.'

'*Lady* Fifi,' corrected the terrier. 'It's *Lady* Fifibelle Champagne-Truffles Gucci-Goo of Tunbridge Wells to you.' She slid down from her mattress throne, clambering over the rubbish piles, and stopped in front of Pup, peering up at him from clouded blue eyes.

Pup glanced at her. She was tiny. Old too. Her fur was long and clumped in thick mats behind her ears and under her belly. She had only a few teeth, and one loose canine tooth stuck out sideways from her lower jaw. A threadbare collar studded with jewels hung loose around her neck. Most of the jewels had fallen out, leaving frayed empty gaps. A growl gargled from Lady Fifi's throat and saliva bubbled either side of her tongue.

Pup backed away from her. She was small, but terrifying.

Not even Frenchi looked her in the eye. 'This is Pup. He needs a place to stay.'

Lady Fifi walked a circle around Pup and then passed right underneath him, her ear tips touching his belly. He tensed up, not daring to move.

She sniffed him and growled. 'What are you?'

Pup glanced at Frenchi, unsure what to say.

'She means what breed are you?' said Frenchi.

'Breed?' said Pup.

'So, I'm a French bulldog,' said Frenchi. 'Merle is a Border collie and Clown is a boxer. Saffy's a Labrador and Reynard is a foxhound. Lady Fifi here is a Jack Russell terrier cross.'

Lady Fifi turned her growl to Frenchi. 'Excuse me!' She snarled, curling her lip, showing her rotten tooth. 'I'm a quarter shih-tzu. My grandfather was Crufts supreme champion.'

'Of course,' said Frenchi.

'I . . . I don't know what I am,' said Pup.

Merle stood up. 'He looks like a mix of dogs. There's German shepherd in him.'

Rex stepped out of the shadows. 'He's too tall and lean. I'm sure there's Belgian Malinois blood in there.'

'What did your mother look like?' asked Clown. 'You must be able to remember her?'

Pup whimpered. These dogs were talking about things he didn't understand. He could only remember a dark place and rough hands before he found his boy. 'I don't know,' he said again.

'He's got the shoulders of a Rottweiler,' said Saffy.

'He's going to be big, whatever,' said Frenchi. 'He might even grow to be as big as Rex.'

'Maybe I'm the same as Rex,' said Pup. 'What breed is he?'

Rex snarled and disappeared into the shadows again.

Pup stared after him. 'What . . .'

Frenchi stepped in front of him and lowered his voice. 'Never ask that question again.'

'Why not?' whispered Pup.

'Just don't,' snapped Frenchi.

A rumbling growl came from the shadows and Pup backed away in silence, wondering what breed Rex was and why no one would talk about it.

'But Pup will be big,' said Lady Fifi. 'Maybe too big. He might draw attention to us. Our greatest risk is being seen.'

'We need another big dog,' argued Frenchi. 'The Sewer Dogs have got Fang. We don't want them taking this place from us.'

Lady Fifi growled. 'We said no more dogs in our pack. We'll have to go further and further to look for food and run the risk of the Snatchers. We can't afford another mouth to feed.'

'He's got nowhere else to go,' said Frenchi.

'You should have thought of that and left him where you found him,' snapped Lady Fifi. 'Maybe you should take him back there.'

'To Dead Dog Alley?' said Frenchi. 'We all know what happens there.'

Pup whimpered. He thought of the humans with the rope and the pole, and the dark street and howling wind. He didn't want to go back.

Saffy stepped forward and licked Pup's ear. 'It's a cold night. And besides, he's only a pup.'

'Exactly,' said Lady Fifi. 'Humans notice pups. We'll be found out. He's too much of a risk.'

'We need him as much as he needs us,' pleaded Frenchi. 'Look at us. Saffy's not strong enough to tip bins over any more. I'm short of breath. Reynard's too scared of his ghosts to help. And you . . .'

Lady Fifi turned to Frenchi and growled. 'What about me?'

Frenchi stared at the ground. 'Well, let's just say you don't get out as much as you used to.'

Lady Fifi pressed her face against Frenchi's, spittle fizzling through her mouth. 'If it wasn't for me, we wouldn't have this place. No one knows the Snatchers like I do. I know how they work and how they think. I keep us safe. Don't forget that.' She spun around, glaring at all the dogs through her cloudy eyes. 'You'd all be in Dogsdoom if it wasn't for me.'

Pup backed away into the shadows, away from Lady Fifi's glare.

'I'll teach Pup how to be a street dog,' said Frenchi. 'He's got nowhere else to go.'

'We'll all help,' promised Saffy.

Merle circled them all again. 'He needs a pack, a family.'

Frenchi glanced at Pup, then lowered his voice, pleading with Lady Fifi. 'We all need to belong. If he doesn't have his human, then he needs to have us. A dog on his own is no dog at all.'

'No dog at all,' repeated Clown.

Lady Fifi clambered back up onto her mattress throne and stared down at them. 'He can stay. For now.' She crawled inside the open handbag and lay down with just the tip of her nose poking out. 'But if he puts a single paw out of line, he's out. Understand?'

Frenchi nodded and pushed Pup into the shadows. 'Best get some sleep,' he said.

Pup watched the other dogs curl up in their separate corners. 'What's Dogsdoom?' he whispered.

'I'm tired,' said Frenchi. 'And you have too many questions. I need to rest.'

'Where do I sleep?' said Pup.

'Anywhere you like,' said Frenchi. He padded over to a pile of newspapers and curled up against the wall. Pup shuffled over and curled next to him, pushing his nose into the warmth of Frenchi's belly.

'Hey, none of that,' said Frenchi. He pushed him away with his feet. 'Find your own space.'

Pup tried to curl next to Frenchi again, but Frenchi growled, a warning grumble deep in his chest.

Pup lay down on the hard floor and shivered. 'I'm cold, Frenchi.'

'Get used to it,' said Frenchi. He turned his back away from Pup.

Pup tucked his nose into his fur. He tried to sleep, but all he could think of was his boy. Everything had changed so quickly. The rain had washed his boy's scent from his fur so all he could remember was the shape of him curled around him.

'I'm lonely, Frenchi,' whispered Pup.

'You have to get used to that too,' said Frenchi. 'You're a street dog now.'

Pup listened to the breathing of the other sleeping dogs and the rumble of trains above. Frenchi yawned and closed his eyes. His paws twitched as he settled into sleep. Pup wanted his boy. He wanted someone to curl up with and hold him safe. He inched closer and closer towards Frenchi, clambered over him and tried to push himself into the space between Frenchi's paws, resting his head on Frenchi's chest. And if Frenchi did wake in the night to find him there, he didn't stir. Pup slept all night curled up against Frenchi's warm body, lulled into sleep by Frenchi's rumbling and snuffling snores.

The Boy

The boy wakes to a cold emptiness beside him.

The house is silent and still. He throws the blanket back and rushes down the stairs, calling for his dog. But when he reaches the kitchen, he just stops and stares. The small red collar that he paid for with his pocket money lies unbuckled on the table. The boy feels an ache deep inside his chest.

He already knows that his dog is gone.

The big man is sitting, eating breakfast. He turns, with a forkful of food, and faces the boy. 'If you've got something to say, say it.'

The boy says nothing. He knows this man is quick with his words and fists.

The boy's mother steps forward. 'We couldn't keep him, love.' She reaches out her hand, but he steps back.

He bites his lip, and blinks back the hot tears that fill his eyes.

The big man turns back to his plate of food. 'If you haven't got anything to say, get out of here.'

The boy hates them. He hates them both. He hates the big man for the man he is, and his mother for betraying him. Fear is rising up inside him. Fear of what the big man might do, but a greater fear of losing his dog for ever.

He stands his ground. 'He was my dog.'

The big man stops eating. 'What did you say?'

The boy says it, louder this time. 'He was my dog.'

The big man slams down his knife and fork and heaves

himself out of his chair, towering over the boy. He pushes his finger into the boy's chest. 'He was never your dog. He belonged to me. He was mine to do with what I wanted.'

The boy backs away, but despite his youth, he knows that you cannot own a dog any more than you can own another person. He knows that when a dog gives you its love, it is a gift.

A gift to be treasured with all your heart and soul.

Chapter 5
REYNARD'S STORY

PUP WOKE TO FRENCHI SHIFTING his weight. He blinked and sat up, trying to remember where he was. The memories of the night before flooded back. Pup wanted his boy. He wanted his boy more than ever. His chest ached with it. His boy would wake to find him gone and they didn't know how to find each other. He looked around the dogs' den. The sound of rain outside had stopped, but damp dripped on the ground from the brick archway above.

Lady Fifi's snoring drifted down from the mattress.

Merle, Clown and Saffy were nowhere to be seen.

Frenchi stretched and yawned. 'You survived the night, then?'

Pup yawned too. The ground had been harder than his boy's soft bed, but Frenchi's body had kept him warm. His fur had dried too. He stood up, arching his back and stretching his legs. 'My boy needs me,' said Pup. 'I've got to go back to him.'

Frenchi stood up and shook himself. 'Go on then,' he said. 'Off you go.'

Pup blinked. 'But which way is home?'

'I wish I could help you,' said Frenchi. 'It could be any-where. I found you in Dead Dog Alley. That's all I know.'

Pup stared at the broken panels at the entrance to the den. His mind blurred with the night before. He tried to think of the map in his mind of home and the park where he played football with his boy. Sometimes the big man took them in

42

the car to the park, but most of the time Pup walked with his boy along the back roads, and through the industrial estate. In his mind he could see the road and the house where his boy lived, but there was a big blank space in his mind between here and there, and he didn't know how to connect the two.

Frenchi sighed. 'The first night is always the worst,' he said. 'It does get easier. The hardest part is accepting you can't ever go back.'

'Ever?' whimpered Pup.

Frenchi licked the sore on his paw. 'In all my dog years I've never heard of it,' he said. 'Even if you could find your way back, what then? You've got to ask yourself why they dumped you. You're a street dog now.'

Pup thought of his boy and felt a black emptiness of loss and loneliness, so deep he couldn't breathe. He felt so far away from his boy. He wanted to feel his boy's arms around him and his paw in the boy's warm hand. A whimper deep in his chest formed into the beginning of a howl that had nowhere to go. His boy wouldn't even hear him.

Frenchi gave him a lick on the face. 'You will get used to it,' he said. 'Trust me. Besides, you've learned the first rule of survival.'

'What's that?' said Pup.

'To find shelter,' said Frenchi. 'Somewhere warm and dry, out of the wind and rain. Know your exits too.' He glanced at the broken wooden panel. 'This place isn't the best. There's no other way out, but it's warm, especially in winter. Fifi led us here and we've never been discovered. Humans don't often come this way.'

Rex opened one eye. 'If the Sewer Dogs find us they'll bring humans and trouble. I've heard they're looking for a safe winter den.'

Pup's stomach rumbled loudly.

'And the second rule of survival is to find food,' said Frenchi. 'Come on, let's go before it gets light. Before the whole city wakes up.'

Reynard, the foxhound, was pacing at the opening to the den, up and down, up and down. He stopped to stick his nose outside and sniffed the air. His tail was rigid in a straight line behind him. 'The night prowlers came by here last night,' he said. 'We're not safe here. We must follow them down into the earth. Deep, deep, deep. The night prowlers can hide us.'

'Night prowlers?' said Pup.

'Foxes,' said Rex. 'Reynard means foxes. Can you smell them? One's been past not long ago.'

Pup sniffed the strange musty animal scent. It was pungent in the still air and Pup wondered what kind of animal could leave such a strong smell. Rex got to his feet and placed himself between Reynard and the opening. 'Don't follow the foxes,' he said to the foxhound. 'Saffy will come back soon, and Saffy wants you to stay here.'

A train rumbled overhead, and Reynard pressed his head against the wall. 'The Huntsman rides an iron mare. He wears black boots and silver spurs.'

'It's just the trains,' said Rex. 'Only the trains.'

'They're in my head,' whimpered Reynard. 'The hooves are stamping in my head.'

44

Rex gently pushed Reynard away from the opening. 'Wait for Saffy. I'll wait with you.'

Reynard curled up in his corner, the whole of his body trembling. He didn't take his eye from the opening. 'Don't let the Huntsman in.'

Frenchi shoved Pup forward. 'Come on. Let's get out of here and find breakfast.'

Rex followed them to the entrance and placed himself on guard in the shadows. 'I won't let Reynard out,' he said. 'The foxes are neither friend nor foe to us, but they won't see him as one of their own and have no desire to protect him.'

'Who's the Huntsman?' whispered Pup. 'Will he find us?'

'It's all in Reynard's head,' said Frenchi, 'or what's left of his head anyway.'

Pup glanced back at Reynard. The damaged side of his face was deep in shadow. 'What happened to him?'

'Reynard came from a hunt kennels in the green lands beyond the city,' said Frenchi. 'He wouldn't chase and kill foxes. And if a foxhound won't kill foxes, he's no use to man.' Frenchi furrowed his brow, choosing his words carefully. 'Let's just say the Huntsman didn't want him around any more.'

Pup shivered. 'Did the Huntsman dump Reynard in the city too?'

'He put a bullet in his head,' said Rex.

'Rex!' growled Frenchi. 'Spare the pup the details.'

'Why not tell him?' said Rex. 'The more he knows about the ways of man, the better his chances of survival.'

'Reynard was lucky,' said Frenchi, turning to Pup.

'Somehow he survived and followed a fox into the city. He thinks they lead to safety, to a place where the Huntsman can't find them.'

'But nowhere is safe,' said Rex, with a low rumbling growl in his throat. 'No human can be trusted. Ever.'

'That's not true,' said Frenchi.

'Really?' growled Rex. 'Name one. Just one. Who would you trust?'

'Come on, Pup,' said Frenchi, ignoring Rex. 'We'd better get going before it gets too light.'

And so Pup followed Frenchi through the broken panel and out into the noise and smells of the vast urban world sprawled out before them.

In the brimming light of a cold grey dawn, one more street dog stepped out into the city.

Chapter 6
THE THIRD RULE
OF SURVIVAL

PUP FOLLOWED FRENCHI TO THE outside world. The last rain-clouds hung like grey rags in the sky against a brightening dawn. The air smelled sharp and fresh, mixed with the tangle of traffic fumes and rain on wet tarmac. The sweet, greasy scent from fast-food stalls drifted on the breeze.

Further along the road a person fumbled with keys to open a garage beneath the railway arches.

'The third rule of survival,' said Frenchi, 'is never to be seen. You have to stay in the shadows. You have to become invisible. That's why we try to go out in the hours of darkness.'

'I'm hungry,' whined Pup.

'I know,' said Frenchi. 'There are a few humans we let see us. I think we might risk seeing the swan lady. She comes at dawn.'

Pup lapped water in a puddle by the road but Frenchi nudged him on. 'It'll make you sick. I'll show you where the safe water is.'

Pup followed Frenchi across a road and through alley-ways until they reached a gap in a fence. The land beyond the fence was dark and green. It smelled of grass and footballs, but it didn't smell quite the same as the park where Pup had played with his boy. This was a different place. Pup padded onto the grass which was soft and cool underfoot.

Frenchi sniffed the ground. 'The Sewer Dogs have been

here. It's a new scent. Maybe from two or three days ago. But they're coming closer.'

'Who are they?' Pup asked.

'Another gang of street dogs,' said Frenchi. 'Their den is in the sewers, but the sewers often flood in the winter, so they're looking for another safe den. They know about us but haven't found us yet.'

Pup shivered. 'Are they dangerous?'

'Their leader is a huge white dog called Fang, with a short temper. So it's best to stay out of their way,' said Frenchi. 'Maybe the most dangerous thing about them is that they're not careful. They're big and noisy, which makes it easy for the Snatchers to find them. We don't want the Snatchers to find us too.'

Pup put his nose to the ground and sniffed around, trying to work out how many different dog scents he could pick up. 'How big is their pack?'

'It changes all the time,' whispered Frenchi. 'Fang is not a dog to argue with. Some try to escape and some just disappear.'

Pup tucked his tail beneath his legs and crept back into the long shadows of a tree. 'Are they still here?'

'It's ok, Pup,' said Frenchi. 'They're long gone. For now. Come on, let's find breakfast.'

Pup followed Frenchi through the park. He felt safer in the darkness between the trees, away from the bright lights of the streets. The park was long and thin with a lake running through the middle of it. In the centre of the lake an island rose above the low mist that hung over the dark water. Ducks and swans rested on the island, their heads tucked beneath their wings in sleep.

'Don't you go chasing them,' said Frenchi, 'or we are in trouble.' He trotted to the lake edge and bent down to lap at the water.

Pup joined him. The water tasted strange, but he was thirsty and drank anyway, taking gulps of the cool water. The city was coming awake around them. The roads hummed with traffic, and beyond the park Pup could see people walking along the pavements. A man on a bicycle whizzed through the park and two joggers ran side by side along the path.

'Keep off the paths,' said Frenchi. 'Humans don't notice much unless it's right in front of their feet.' He led the way under the hanging branches of rhododendron bushes further up the lake edge and found a dry patch amongst the waxy leaves scattered on the ground.

'What are we doing?' Pup whispered.

'Waiting for breakfast,' said Frenchi. He looked up at the sky. Rays of sunlight reflected gold on office windows. The sun was rising above the city. 'Not long now.'

Pup sat next to Frenchi, but impatience tugged at him. He chewed at a stick on the ground, ripping the end into shreds.

'Here she comes,' said Frenchi, looking out from beneath the branches.

Pup looked too. An elderly lady was walking slowly along the path around the lake, pulling a trolley behind her. The wheels squeaked and rattled as she made her way steadily forward. On the island, the birds heard her and looked up, flapping their wings and stretching. The swans came first, waddling to the water's edge and launching in. They glided across through the thin veil of mist, the water rippling out behind them. The ducks followed noisily, quacking and quarrelling, racing each other to reach the lake edge. The birds gathered around the lady. The ducks fussed at her feet while the swans stood tall, stretching their necks and waggling their tails, waiting for breakfast. The lady stooped to open her trolley and threw bread for them.

'OK, do as I do,' said Frenchi, wriggling out from the bush. 'And whatever you do, don't chase the birds.'

Frenchi trotted to the edge of the lake a little way from the frenzy of swans and ducks and sat down and waited. Pup sat beside him, resisting the urge to charge into the group of birds.

'Well, if it isn't my old friend,' said the lady, spying Frenchi. 'I haven't seen you for a while. And you've brought another friend with you too.'

Frenchi sat back on his haunches and put a front paw in the air. Pup sat with his paws together and tipped his head to the side.

The swan lady chuckled and pulled a bag out of her trolley. 'As you've asked so nicely you can have some of my bacon roll.' She pulled apart the bread and greasy bacon and threw the pieces to the waiting dogs.

Pup wolfed his down and sat, paws together asking for more.

'You're a young one, aren't you?' she said, taking a step closer. She put her hand out and Pup leaned towards her. He wanted to feel her hands stroke his head and scratch behind his ear like his boy used to do.

'Don't let her touch you,' Frenchi warned softly.

Pup backed away, but he sat down again, wagging the tip of his tail.

'A shy one,' said the lady. 'And you look hungry to me.' She threw the rest of her bread roll for Pup and he wolfed that down too.

'Come on,' said Frenchi. 'That's our lot. Let's get out of here.'

Pup followed, but turned to look back at the swan lady. She smiled and gave a little wave.

'I'm still hungry,' said Pup.

'It's getting too light,' said Frenchi. 'We need to get back.'

Frenchi trotted away into the shadows, but Pup noticed a man walking alongside the lake, eating something from a paper bag. The smell of hot bread drifted on the air. Pup couldn't resist it. He ran down to the water's edge and sat waiting like he had done with the swan lady. The man stopped and stared at Pup for a while, then crouched down, his arm outstretched. Pup wanted to meet him. Maybe he knew his boy. Maybe he could take him back to his boy. He was about to step forward when Frenchi jostled between him and the man.

'Come on,' growled Frenchi, pushing Pup. 'I said, get out of here. Didn't you hear me say we have to be invisible? We can't be seen.'

Pup trotted along beside Frenchi. 'But we let the swan lady see us.'

'She's different,' said Frenchi, slowing down to a walk. He was huffing and puffing and out of breath. 'If we let other humans see us, they call the Snatchers. We can't risk it. It'll be over for us. They'll take us to Dogsdoom.'

'We can't let any other humans near us?' whimpered Pup. He thought of his boy. He thought of never seeing him again. 'Ever?'

Frenchi sat down in a puddle and licked his paw. 'No,' he said. 'Once we become street dogs, we are not part of their world any more.'

Pup walked back in silence behind Frenchi. Everything had changed. There was a great divide between dogs and men.

Pup didn't want to be a street dog.

He didn't want this new world.

He just wanted to be curled up with his boy.

But this was his life now.

And there seemed no hope of ever seeing his boy again.

Chapter 7
INTO THE
SHADOWS

By the time Frenchi and Pup reached the Railway Den, the sun had risen, but the railway arches were still in deep shadow. A van had parked beside one of the garages, but there was no one to be seen. Frenchi looked around before slipping through the broken panel into the den.

Merle circled them. 'One, two, three, four, five, six, seven and me. All here,' she said.

'Did you find food?' asked Saffy.

'Not much,' said Frenchi. He turned to speak up to Lady Fifi. 'The Sewer Dogs are coming closer. They left their scent at the park.'

'We'll have to keep away from the park then, for a while,' growled Lady Fifi. 'There will be Snatchers about. No one goes out until dark-fall tonight.'

Pup whimpered.

Frenchi looked across at Lady Fifi. 'Pup's only had a mouthful of food. And I'm guessing he didn't eat much yesterday. He'll need something. I'll take him to the shop bins. They're not far.'

'He'll have to wait,' said Fifi. 'It's too light outside.'

'He's just a pup,' said Frenchi. 'Everyone else ate last night. I'll take him out. We won't be long.'

'Too risky,' said Fifi. 'Besides, you said yourself you can't tip bins. Look at you, Frenchi. You can't even run without collapsing.'

Frenchi tried to stop panting, but he snorted and snuffed

and couldn't get air through his nose, so he opened his mouth to breathe again.

'Why can't you breathe, Frenchi?' said Pup.

'Born like it,' said Frenchi. 'I'd love a long snout like yours, but humans want us French bulldogs to look like this.'

'They don't want you to breathe?' said Pup.

Rex stepped forward. 'They don't think about that. Humans think he's cute. He looks like a human baby to them, with his big eyes and small nose. They want cute dogs. They only think about what they want.'

'Cute?' said Pup, trying not to sound surprised. He looked at Frenchi's squashed face and folds of crusted skin. Blobs of yellow snot bubbled at his narrow nostrils. 'But you can't breathe.'

'I get by,' said Frenchi, his tongue hanging out. 'I get by.'

Lady Fifi climbed down from her mattress. 'There are places humans can make you better,' she said. 'I've been there. My leg was broken, and they fixed it. They stick things in you, and you hate it, but it does make you better.'

Frenchi sighed. 'The first humans I had took me to a place like that once, but they dumped me when I started having more problems.'

'It's what they do,' growled Rex. 'You just watch them. They throw everything away when it's no use to them.'

Pup's stomach rumbled again.

Rex glared at him. 'Is your stomach going to rumble like that all day long?'

'I'm hungry,' whimpered Pup.

Rex got up and shook himself. 'If Fifi will let us, *I'll*

take you out to find some food, just to keep your stomach quiet.'

Lady Fifi walked a circle around Pup. 'You can go with Rex, but do everything he tells you to. Do you understand? Or you put all of us in danger.'

'I'll come as well,' said Frenchi, standing up too.

Rex stretched, arching his back, getting ready to run. 'We need speed,' he said. 'I'm sorry, Frenchi. I think you'll have to stay behind.'

Frenchi sat back down and turned to Pup. 'Go with Rex. Do what he says.'

Pup looked warily at Rex, but Rex was already up and sniffing the air.

'It's not far,' Rex said.

Lady Fifi followed them to the entrance. 'Know your exits. If in doubt, drop everything and run.'

Pup trotted after Rex. It was hard to keep up with him. Frenchi had a slow waddling trot, but Rex loped in long easy strides. Despite his size, he somehow seemed to fold into the shadows. No one noticed him pass. Pup followed him along roads and through alleyways until Rex stopped at the gates to a yard that smelled deliciously of food. There was a building with huge glass windows and aisles of meat and vegetables and packets of all shapes and sizes. 'People get food in these places,' said Rex. 'It's hard to get inside, but they put food they don't want in those big bins.'

The back of the food store was strewn with paper and rubbish. Hot steam came from a vent in the side of the building and Pup licked his lips at the smell of warm bread. He followed Rex to the bins in a corner. Some were firmly closed, but others were bursting full.

Rex walked along beside them, standing up on his hind legs and looking in. He sniffed several times. 'This is a good one. We'll have one chance. Once it comes down, grab what you can. And if I bark "run", then you start running and you don't stop. Understand?'

Pup watched Rex reach up on his hind legs to pull at one of the bins. Its wheels caught on a kerb and it rocked backwards and forwards until it tipped and came crashing down, the sound echoing from the walls around the yard. Cabbages and apples spilled out and rolled on the ground. Pup's nose led him to a meaty scent beneath piles of packaging. He began rummaging, following the smell.

'Let's go,' said Rex, reaching for a loaf of bread.

Pup's nose found a pack of sausages. He dived for it and grabbed it in his teeth, feeling proud of his find. He had found his first meal. Maybe he could learn to be a street dog. Maybe Frenchi would be proud of him too.

'Hey!' A man's voice came from somewhere behind the bins. 'Hey! Stop!'

Pup's heart pounded in his chest. He ran, following Rex. Footsteps seemed to be right behind him. He glanced back to see a man running towards him. The man was gaining on him with big human strides, even though he only had two legs. Pup tried to run faster but his big puppy paws tangled up and he tripped, rolling over and over, dropping his precious sausages.

He forgot Rex's words. He forgot what Lady Fifi had told him. His stomach cried out for food. All he could think about was the sausages lying in the dirt. He scrambled up and lunged for them.

Maybe if he hadn't turned to look behind he wouldn't have tripped. Maybe if he'd picked himself up and left the sausages, he would have got away. But the man was faster. Pup felt hands around him, big hands that held him tight and lifted him up by the scruff of his neck. He dropped the sausages and twisted and turned in the man's hands, but he couldn't get away. The man's fingers dug deep into his skin.

Fear tore through him.

This was all his fault.

He hadn't listened to Rex.

He hadn't listened to Lady Fifi.

He hadn't followed the rules.

He'd only been a street dog for less than a day, and now he'd let himself be caught.

Chapter 8
THE LUPUS BOND

Pup wriggled and clawed with his feet, but the man's hands held him tightly. Pup called out to Rex, a high-pitched yelp and cry. Rex spun round and dropped his bread loaf by the gateway.

'Rex!' yelped Pup.

Everything happened in a blur after that. Rex was bounding across towards him, his hackles raised and his lips peeled back showing his teeth. A snarling growl came from somewhere deep in Rex's chest.

'Hey, Javid!' shouted the man.

Another man appeared behind them and he kicked out at Rex, but Rex dodged the kick.

'Rex!' yelped Pup, as the man clung onto him.

Rex leaped forward, sinking his teeth into the man's arm, and the man fell, releasing Pup in a tangle of man and dogs. But Rex didn't stop. It was as if something wild had possessed him. He didn't stop biting and shaking the man. Spit and blood flew through the air. The man curled up into a ball to protect himself, but Rex kept up his savage attack.

Pup scrambled to his feet. All he could think about was getting away. The sausages were right beside him, so he snatched them and ran. He ran and ran out into the street, the last sound he heard being the thump of a boot against a dog's chest, and Rex's anguished cry.

Pup wasn't even sure if he was going the right way. He just ran, letting his feet take him. His heart pounded inside his chest. Doorways and parked cars passed in a blur beside him; a car screeched to a stop when he ran across a road. He kept running until he heard the clicking of nails on the pavement behind him. Rex appeared beside him, and Pup noticed he was limping.

'Keep going. Don't stop,' said Rex, leading the way.

Rex slipped under a wire fence and trotted across a yard and out to a street on the other side, then limped down steps to the road with the railway arches. Rex sat in the shadows until two men had walked past the Railway Den, then he set off. 'Come on, let's get back now. Be quick. Don't be seen.'

Pup followed Rex into the den and the other dogs crowded around them.

'One, two, three, four, five, six, seven and me,' said Merle, circling Pup. 'All here.'

Saffy pushed her nose into Pup's fur. 'I smell humans.'

Frenchi shuffled forward. 'What happened?'

'We're OK,' said Rex, licking his paw. 'Close call, that's all.'

Pup had already torn into his packet of sausages and was chomping them, saliva and greasy meat dribbling down his chin.

Lady Fifi stirred from her mattress and made her way down. She sniffed at the sausages and gave a trilling growl.

Pup lowered his head over his prize of sausages and growled back.

'So, the pup's got some spark,' said Fifi, walking a circle around him. 'That's good. He'll need it.'

'Let Lady Fifi have a sausage,' whispered Frenchi. 'It's the rules.'

Pup tried to turn his back on the others, keeping up his puppy growl, guarding his sausages.

Saffy lay a paw on Pup's back. 'Lady Fifi can't get food herself, but she knows how to keep us safe.'

Pup reluctantly backed away from the sausages and watched as Fifi pulled one out and returned to her mattress.

Rex limped over and took one too.

'We work together as a pack,' said Frenchi. 'It's how we all survive.'

Pup stared at the remaining sausages. He nudged one to Frenchi. 'Do you want one too?'

'Thank you,' said Frenchi, taking one too. 'I've a weak spot for sausages. You finish the rest.'

Pup ate them, gulping them down just in case Frenchi wanted another, then he licked the packet clean.

Frenchi waited for him to finish. 'So, what happened?'

'I got caught,' whimpered Pup, wincing at the memory of the rough hands digging in to him.

Frenchi pushed his nose into Pup's fur, smelling the scent of human hands. 'How did you get away?'

'We got away,' snapped Rex. 'That's all you need to know.'

'Rex bit the man,' said Pup. 'He bit him again and again.'

All the other dogs stopped and turned to Rex.

'I had to,' said Rex with a low growl. 'There was no other way.'

Pup puffed out his chest. 'And I'm going to do the same if they catch me again. I'm going to bite and bite until they let me go.'

He wasn't expecting to be knocked off his feet, but Frenchi butted his head into Pup's chest, and left him gasping on the floor.

'Never,' growled Frenchi, 'never ever bite a human. Do you understand?' Pup tried to get to his feet, but Frenchi stood over him. 'Do you understand?'

'But why not?' said Pup. 'What if they try to grab you?'

'If you bite,' said Frenchi, 'you break the sacred bond of Lupus. Once it's broken, it can never be mended.'

'The bond of Lupus?' said Pup.

Frenchi stared at him. 'Didn't your mother tell you the story of the Great Sky Wolf when you were a wee pup drinking her milk?'

'I . . . I can't remember,' said Pup.

'Weren't you listening?' said Frenchi harshly. 'It's the most important story of all.'

'Hush now,' said Saffy, pushing herself between Pup and Frenchi. 'You know not all mothers get to keep their pups long enough to tell them stories.'

Frenchi backed away. 'I'm sorry, Saffy.' He lowered his head. 'I'm sorry, Pup. I forgot.' He licked at the sore on his left front paw and Pup began to notice he did it when he was anxious and worried. Maybe it was his worry-paw.

'The old stories are stupid stories anyway,' growled Rex. 'They are made up by man to control us, to make us scared of freedom.'

Saffy shook her head. 'The old stories are there to give us faith,' she said.

'Faith!' growled Rex. 'I've been around humans all my

life. I've been kicked by them, starved by them and left for dead by them. There's no good in any of them. They build your hopes up and then destroy them. We're best off without them. I have no faith in man.'

'We share our ancestry,' said Saffy. 'The Lupus bond binds us with them.'

'As a servant,' said Rex, pulling back his teeth in a snarl.

'What is the Lupus bond?' asked Pup.

'I shall tell you the story,' said Saffy. 'For every dog must know it and decide their own destiny. It is a story of our bond with man. This story may one day save your life.'

The other dogs crept a bit closer to listen, because dogs, like humans, love to hear stories. They feel the rhythm of the words, and somewhere deep inside of them they remember the dark nights around an open fire and feel the need for the shared togetherness. Stories bind and keep them, and remind them who they are.

Pup curled up against Frenchi's pudgy folds of skin, his stomach feeling full and warm. Reynard sat beside Saffy and let her wash his face, then he too curled up. Merle moved closer and put her head on her paws and Lady Fifi put her head over the top of the mattress to listen. Even Clown settled down. Only Rex stayed in the shadows, but Pup could see his ears twitching as he listened to her story.

And so Saffy told the story of the Great Sky Wolf, the first story of the bond between man and dog. Even though the other dogs knew it by heart, they listened, wanting to find more meaning and hope within the words. They listened again to the story of the first dog, Sirius, and how he and man formed a bond so strong it held them beyond death. She sighed and finished the story. 'So, dear Pup, you must know Sirius died for us. He gave his life so that we might be loved by man.'

Pup whined, thinking about his boy's arms around him.

'It's why we don't bite humans,' said Merle quietly. 'It's a sacred bond. If we bite, we break that bond and lose their trust.'

Rex jumped up and barked. 'Sirius betrayed us. We would have been better off with the wolves. Humans don't deserve our trust. All they know is cruelty.'

'The Huntsman took my eye,' whimpered Reynard.

Saffy sighed. 'Humans are capable of great cruelty,' she said. 'I know. I have seen it too. They kept me in a cage having litters and litters of puppies I could not keep. When I got sick they dumped me in Dead Dog Alley. Had it not been for Frenchi finding me that night, I would not be here.'

'And you still have faith in humans after that?' growled Rex.

Reynard pushed his head against Saffy. 'Don't let the Huntsman in.'

Saffy licked Reynard's ears. 'It is hard to believe humans are capable of love when you haven't felt it. But they are. I know they are. I once belonged to a family.' She closed her eyes, remembering. 'Long, long ago, for I am an old dog now, there was a golden place. I was stolen from that place and from those people who loved me. But I still remember the feel of their hands stroking my ears. I remember running along white sand with the sun on my fur and the wind blowing back my ears. I remember lying beside a roaring fire, with a wild storm outside, safe beside my humans. So when I feel angry, I think of those people I was stolen from. Because the story of the Great Sky Wolf is not a story about keeping faith in humans. It is about keeping faith in ourselves. We must keep faith in that strong bond and in the love we have for humans. We are not their servants. We are their guides.'

Lady Fifi gave her trilling growl. 'I agree with Rex. The old stories are just stories. The world is no longer made from ice and fire. We are nothing to humans any more. We are playthings. We have to look after each other now. It's how we survive. Maybe we should tell Pup the real reason why we don't bite humans. Maybe we should tell him what happens to forbidden breeds like Rex.'

'No,' said Saffy quietly. 'Don't tell him that.'

Pup was aware of the silence of the other dogs, as if Lady Fifi had spoken words that should have been left unspoken.

'He'll have to know sometime,' said Fifi.

Rex growled a low growl that ended in a whine of anguish.

Frenchi shuffled uneasily. 'Maybe another day, Fifi. We are all tired and need some sleep.'

Pup curled up next to Frenchi and looked out through the broken panel. A shaft of daylight cut through into the den. Sounds drifted inside of the traffic and rumble of trains, and people's voices.

Worry twitched Pup's paws. 'What was Fifi saying?' he whispered to Frenchi. 'What's a forbidden breed?'

Frenchi lowered his voice. 'Humans think Rex is a dangerous dog. His breed is outlawed.'

Rex growled from the shadows. 'I'm an outcast. Bred to be a fighter. Bred to be a monster. But the only true monsters I've seen are men.'

'What do humans do to forbidden breeds?' whimpered Pup. 'What do they do to us if we bite a person?'

Frenchi closed his eyes and shuddered. 'Sleep now, Pup. Just sleep.'

But Pup took a long time to go to sleep. He watched the shaft of sunlight cross the den as the sun crossed from east to west in the sky. There was so much to know. There was so much he didn't know. It seemed that dogs could be trusted. They told the truth. But humans were very different.

Doubt crept into his mind. Maybe his boy had already forgotten all about him.

Maybe Rex was right, and humans couldn't be trusted at all.

Chapter 9
TRUST YOUR NOSE

PUP WOKE WHILE ALL THE other dogs slumbered. Frenchi's soft snores rumbled beside him. Something was different. Pup sat up and stared into the gloom. The shadows seemed to shift and move and then Pup saw him. There was a person in the den, a boy, sitting on the ground with a football at his side.

Pup glanced at the other dogs but they were fast asleep, even Rex.

There was something familiar about the boy, the shape of him, the way he tipped his head to the side to look at Pup.

'My boy?' whimpered Pup.

The boy smiled and held his arms out.

'My boy,' cried Pup. He leaped to his feet. *His* boy. *His* boy was here. Pup knew he would find him. How could he have doubted humans only the night before? He should have known. *His* boy would always find him. Pup didn't want to wake Frenchi, so he slowly wriggled from under Frenchi's paws and then trotted over towards his boy. But the boy had turned his back and he slipped outside through the broken panel.

'Wait,' yipped Pup, running after him.

He slipped through the entrance too, but he wasn't on the road beneath the railway arches any more – he was in the park where he once played football with his boy. Shafts of bright sunlight slanted through the trees, throwing long shadows across the ground. It was busy in the park. Pup caught glimpses of his boy slipping through the crowds.

'Wait,' yipped Pup again. His boy didn't seem to hear. Pup yipped and yipped and ran after him, his legs moving as fast as they could. He was running and running, his feet spinning across the ground, but however fast he ran, his boy seemed to be getting further and further away. Pup threw his head back and did what he did best. He took a deep breath and howled, a long rising howl for his boy to hear. A howl of fear of losing his boy again.

'Pup! Wake up!'

Pup felt Frenchi's nose against him and he opened his eyes. He was no longer in the park, but back in the den, in the darkness, with Frenchi, Saffy, Reynard and Merle all staring at him.

Frenchi nudged him again. 'You OK?'

Pup sat up and looked around. 'My boy was here.'

Frenchi looked at the others and saw their concerned faces.

'I saw him,' said Pup. 'I saw him here. He went outside.'

Saffy sat down beside him. 'He's not here. He's in the place you go to in your sleep,' she said gently. 'It's not part of this world.'

'But I saw him,' said Pup. 'He was here. Then we were in a park and I lost him.'

'So how did you end up back here?' said Frenchi.

Pup looked at them all. 'I don't know, but I know I saw him.'

'You were dreaming,' said Merle. 'You were paddling your feet and howling in your sleep.'

'But I saw him,' whimpered Pup. 'It must be real.'

73

'There are ways to tell what's real or not,' said Frenchi. 'Did you smell him? Can you smell him now?'

Pup sniffed deeply. He got up and sniffed around the ground and the entrance, but he couldn't find any scent of his boy.

Frenchi licked Pup's ears. 'Trust your nose. A dog always trusts his nose. It won't let you down.'

Pup stared at the floor. He felt the loss of his boy all over again. His heart ached with it. He curled up in the shadows and tucked his nose into his fur. He wanted to go back to sleep and find his boy and never wake up. He closed his eyes and wished he could just disappear into the darkness.

'Hey, Pup,' said Frenchi. 'I think we should go and find some food soon. The sun has set and dark is falling.'

Pup just tucked his nose deeper into his fur. He didn't want to go anywhere.

Merle circled around him. 'The pup needs some play-time,' she said. 'Why don't we take him to the south bank of the river?'

'And play night thieves,' said Clown. 'My favourite game.'

Rex glared at them. 'Count me out. I'm not playing any games with humans.'

'We'll take him,' said Merle.

Clown sprung about at the thought of it, skipping circles around Pup. 'People sit outside at tables full of food. So much food for the taking.'

Frenchi chewed at his worry-paw. 'I'll come too,' he said. 'We don't want anyone to get close to him.'

Merle trotted to the entrance and put her nose out,

sniffing the air. 'These are the nights when the humans are full of song and wine.'

Clown bounced after Merle, but Pup didn't move. Pup wanted to fall asleep and find his boy in the world that was not this world.

'Come on,' said Frenchi, pushing Pup to his feet. 'We must learn to live with what we have. It does no good to lose yourself in dreams.'

The Boy

The boy scrapes at the wet clay, marking the pattern of fur in the remembered shape of his dog. He is good with his hands. These are the only school lessons he likes, where he can create something from clay or metal or wood.

He fires the small clay dog in the kiln, and when it has been cooled, he holds it up to the light. The shiny black glaze sparkles as if it is a night sky sprinkled with stars. The boy will keep it safe in his pocket, and hold it tight in his warm human hand.

Every day he walks across the park, slowing his steps along the path where he once ran with Pup through the dappled sunlight of the summer. But it is late autumn now. The trees have lost their coat of leaves, and their bare branches stand stark against a colourless sky.

The boy sits on a bench and pulls his hood up against the biting wind. He will sit here waiting, and leave a small crust of bread beneath the bench, holding onto the hope of Pup returning.

He curls his fingers around the small clay dog and closes his eyes. In his dreams he sees his dog bounding across the grass towards him. He holds onto that dream, wanting to lose himself in a world that is not this world. But he knows he cannot go there, however much he wants to.

He opens his eyes, and Pup is gone.

The small clay dog and the memories are all he owns.

Chapter 10

NIGHT THIEVES AND TABLE DANCERS

CLOWN BOUNCED MAD CIRCLES AROUND Pup. 'The night is young and there are sausages for the taking. Why stay here when there are sausages calling us?'

'Beefburgers,' said Merle. 'Food. Everywhere.'

Pup tucked his nose deeper into his fur and tried to ignore Clown.

'Come on,' barked Clown, pushing his nose beneath Pup. 'Tonight we are night thieves, table dancers and mischief-makers.'

Pup found himself hassled to his feet and shoved outside. He followed Merle and Clown away from the Railway Den, with Frenchi huffing and puffing behind.

Merle set off at a fast collie-trot, head down, ears flat against her head and her tail low and slightly curled. Clown gambolled after her, jumping to catch moths that fluttered to the street lights, and Pup stayed close to Frenchi, hoping Frenchi could keep up.

Merle led them to stone steps going down to the river's edge. The tide was out, and the river was low. The bright city lights reflected in the pools and puddles between the dark mounds of the mud banks.

Merle sniffed the air. 'Night prowlers!' she said. 'Foxes have been this way.'

Pup recognized the musty scent of fox. In the soft light of twilight, he could see the shape of one trotting along the shoreline. Its head was low to the ground, sniffing, and its

78

long bushy tail flowed out behind it. It stopped and turned to face Pup, its eyes reflecting the light.

Pup stared at it. He had never seen a fox before. It looked a bit like a dog, but there was something different about it, something fleeting and unreachable, like a solid shadow.

'Are foxes like us?' asked Pup.

'They have the body of a dog, but the eyes of a cat,' said Merle. 'They are wild-folk. They have no bond with man or us.'

'That's why they're fun to chase,' laughed Clown, and he bounded down the steps onto the riverbank, his long legs leaping across the mud. The fox turned and slipped into the shadows and was gone.

'Where'd he go?' said Clown, spinning around and sniffing the air.

Frenchi nudged Pup and pointed his nose to the river. 'They're clever, they are. They slip away as soon as you see them.'

Pup could see the fox in the shallow water, swimming parallel to the shore. It pulled itself out of the river a little further down, shook its coat and trotted on downriver.

'Come on,' said Merle. 'We can walk along the riverbank while the tide's out. It's safer down here. The only humans I've seen down here are night thieves too, and they don't have much interest in us.'

The mud was soft under Pup's paws and it seemed safe and hidden away from the noise and lights of the roads above.

Clown trotted ahead, then stopped. He lifted a paw and

pointed his nose to some gulls standing at the water's edge. 'Come on, Pup,' he said. 'Let's have some fun.' He began stalking the gulls, walking slowly, his head and body low to the ground. Pup followed close behind. One of the gulls turned its head and watched them with its beady eye.

'Now!' barked Clown, springing forward. He ran ahead, chasing the gulls up into the sky, where they wheeled and mewled angrily at him. Pup joined in, jumping up, trying to knock them out of the air as they dive-bombed him. Then Clown ran wild circles around Pup, scampering with his tail tucked beneath him.

Pup chased after him, letting out all the energy that had been coiled inside of him. It felt good to run and leap for the sheer joy of being alive. For a brief moment, Pup forgot all about his boy and being hungry. He just bounded with Clown, splashing through the cold water, allowed, fleetingly, to be a puppy again, without a care in the world. Clown tripped Pup with his paw and they went tumbling in the soft mud, ending up in a heap on the ground.

Clown stood up and shook himself. 'Come on, there's more fun to come. Let's join the others.'

Pup trotted alongside him. 'Why are you a street dog, Clown? Why didn't your humans want you?'

Clown slowed down. 'My fault,' he whined. 'I can't stop playing. It's my feet, see! They just want to keep moving.'

'I like playing with you,' said Pup.

'Thank you, Pup,' said Clown. 'I like playing with you, too.' He stopped to shake the mud and water from his coat.

Merle gave a sharp bark to call them on.

'Doesn't Merle like to play with you?' asked Pup.

'She's a collie,' whispered Clown. 'She always needs a job to do. That's why her humans dumped her. She was shut in a room all day. A brain like hers has got to have something to do. She ripped up and chewed everything to stop the boredom.'

Pup and Clown caught up with Frenchi and Merle where they were waiting for them at the bottom of some narrow steps cut into the wall. The steps were green and slimed with weed. Rusted chains hung down, festooned with buoys.

'Up here,' Merle said. She turned to Pup. 'We are the night thieves tonight.'

'And table dancers,' said Clown as he trotted up the steps, his tongue lolling out. 'This is where the fun begins.'

Merle sniffed the air. 'The first rule of theft is distraction. You and Clown provide the distraction while I slip in and do the taking. The second rule is to create chaos wherever you can.'

'And the third rule is to run,' said Clown.

'If we need to get away, come down here,' said Merle. 'We'll use the riverbank before the tide comes in.'

'I'll wait for you here,' said Frenchi. 'I'm not so fast on my feet.' He turned to Pup. 'Stick with Merle and Clown. Watch and learn. When they're together, no one's supper is safe!'

Pup followed Merle and Clown up onto the street. There were so many people. Cafés and restaurants spilled their tables outside. Bright lights were strung along the street and music and chatter filled the air. People sat at the tables in their coats, laughing and talking.

It was so busy that no one noticed the three dogs slipping through the crowds. The smell of spices and meats drifted on the air. Pup pushed his nose in a discarded packet on the ground. He pulled out a half-eaten burger and ate it.

'Leave the onions,' said Merle. 'They'll make you sick.'

Clown rummaged in another pile of rubbish and chewed on chicken bones.

But Merle had her eyes on a bigger prize. 'Let's show Pup how we do it,' she said. She was looking over at a table outside a restaurant. A mother, father and two young children were being served by a waiter who put down plates and a rack of spare ribs.

Clown drooled long strings of saliva when he saw the meat. 'Come on, Pup. Do as I do. We're the distraction.'

Pup followed close behind Clown and trotted over to the family. Clown sat a little distance from the children and put his head on one side. Pup sat next to him, eyeing the people warily.

The girl pointed and squealed.

'Don't touch him, honey,' said the mum. 'He's not clean.'

'Can I feed them?' asked the boy.

Clown lay down and rolled on his back, waving his legs in the air, and the boy laughed and leaned over to look at him. The mother took out her phone to take a photo and that's when Merle made her move.

Merle had slipped through the shadows, and when the humans were distracted by Clown and Pup, she put her paws on the table, gently took the whole rack of ribs in her mouth and slipped back into the shadows.

'That's how to do it,' said Clown, seeing Merle slink away. 'Come on. Time to go.'

Pup followed Clown through the jostling crowds, looking back to see the angry father gesticulating to the waiter and wondering where his meal had gone. They joined Merle who had stopped in an alleyway, and sat with her, tearing into the spare ribs.

'Let's do it again,' said Merle, licking her lips. 'We'll take some food back for the others.'

She led them further along the market where tables and chairs had been placed outside a burger bar. Pup and Clown approached a couple and sat beside them, paws together. Burgers, chips and drinks were on the table. Pup knew what he was doing now. He sat up and begged with his paws in the air.

The woman smiled and broke off a bit of burger and held it out for Pup.

'Don't get in touching distance,' warned Clown.

Pup just stared at the offered burger, saliva drooling from his mouth.

'C'mon, boy,' the woman said, reaching forward.

The man laughed. 'He's not having any of mine. I paid good money for that.'

But he didn't see Merle slip a circle around him. She put her paws on the table and grabbed a burger. But the table wasn't sturdy enough to hold her weight and it came crashing down.

'Hey!' yelled the man. 'Grab that dog!' He lobbed a bread roll at the dogs, and Merle leaped up and caught in it the air. 'Stop them!'

'Run!' laughed Clown. 'I'll create chaos.'

And Pup ran, following Merle to the steps down to the riverbank. He stopped to look back and saw Clown bouncing from table to table, food and insults flying in the air.

When Clown joined Pup and Merle on the riverbank, he had a whole burger in his jaws.

'Come on,' said Merle. 'There's not much time.'

The tide had turned and there was only a narrow strip of riverbank between the river and the wall. The incoming tide sucked and gurgled in the darkness. Pup's paws sunk deep into the soft mud and sometimes he had to paddle through water. A passing boat sent a wave of water that washed over him, and he struggled to trot to keep up.

'We need to get up to street level now,' said Frenchi, leading the way up from the river. Their route home was blocked by a fast road with cars and lorries streaming by in both directions.

'I haven't been this way before,' said Merle. 'How do we cross?'

'We don't go across. We go under,' said Frenchi, trotting down steps to a dark tunnel beneath the road.

The tunnel was dimly lit, and smelled stale and musty. There were humans in the tunnel. Some humans were sitting with their backs against the tunnel walls and some were lying down with blankets wrapped around them. There were dogs next to some of the humans too, that eyed the street dogs warily. Pup couldn't help staring at them.

A small brown terrier raised her head from the end of a

blanket. She showed her teeth at Pup. 'Keep walking,' she growled.

Pup looked away and moved closer to Frenchi.

One young man was sitting with his head in his hands, with half a loaf of bread beside him.

Pup drooled. He hadn't brought anything back for Lady Fifi or the others at the Railway Den. He was a night thief now. He wanted to prove to Frenchi what he could do. He hung back behind the others and when they had passed the man, Pup yipped and made his move. 'Watch me,' he barked. He made a sprint for the bread, grabbing it in his mouth and running towards them.

Frenchi stood in front of him. 'Put that back now,' he barked.

Pup looked back at the man. 'Why? We're night thieves now.'

'We don't take from the street people,' growled Frenchi.

'Why not?' said Pup.

'Because they're like us,' said Merle. 'They don't have food of their own.'

Frenchi pushed Pup roughly towards the man and Pup dropped the bread at his feet.

'So, you're not a thief?' said the man to Pup. He broke a piece of bread and threw it for Frenchi and Pup.

Pup went to take it, but Frenchi nudged him away. 'Don't!' he said. 'Don't have anything to do with these people.'

'Why not?' Pup asked. 'Do they . . . catch dogs?'

Merle shook her head. 'Do you see any of their dogs on leads? Their dogs choose to stay with them.'

Pup followed Frenchi along the tunnel. 'But that man offered his food to us.'

'Leave it,' said Frenchi.

'But why?' insisted Pup, tugging at the tip of Frenchi's stubby tail. 'They have other dogs with them. Are they nasty humans? Are they cruel?'

Frenchi spun around and growled in Pup's face. 'Because if you get close to them, they will break your heart,' he snapped.

Pup watched Frenchi trot away by himself.

'Frenchi!' called Pup.

But Merle held Pup back. 'Leave him, Pup. There are things in Frenchi's past he doesn't talk about.'

Pup stared after him. He wondered what Frenchi dreamed about when he whined and paddled his legs in sleep. Were there memories that haunted Frenchi too?

By the time Pup arrived back in the den, he was cold and tired, but he was no longer hungry. Merle and Clown dropped the burgers for the other dogs to eat.

Saffy gave Pup a lick. 'You're back.'

Reynard sniffed at Pup. 'Did you see the night prowlers?'

Pup nodded. 'By the riverside.'

'We must follow them,' said Reynard. He rubbed at the scar on his damaged face. 'They can hide us from the Huntsman. We must follow them, deep, deep, deep into the ground.'

'You're safe here,' said Saffy, nudging Reynard into the shadows.

Rex took half a burger in his mouth and carried it up

to Lady Fifi, who was struggling to stand up. She munched with her toothless gums on the soft meat and bread, and then curled back into her handbag.

As the pack settled down, Pup sidled up to Frenchi, curling up against his warm back.

He tried to forget his boy who had come to him in a dream. Dreams were the past, the remembered things, but they were unreachable. He would try to forget all about his boy. Because that was a place he could never return to.

He belonged to this pack, in this den, in this city.

This is how he would survive.

With Frenchi, Fifi, Merle, Saffy, Reynard, Clown and Rex.

He was a night thief.

And he had so much to learn.

This was his world.

He was a street dog now.

Chapter 11
HANDBAG HOME

As THE MONTHS PASSED BY and the cold creeping winter turned into spring, Pup grew into his long legs. He was a year old now and had reached his full height, standing shoulder to shoulder with Rex. He was still lean and had the gangly legs of youth, but he was strong and had learned quickly how to survive.

He was a street dog now. Part of a pack, and loyal to the pack. Sometimes his boy came to him in his dreams, but he seemed like a distant memory, like remembered sunshine from another summer. Pup knew they were just dreams. He could only catch fleeting glimpses of his boy and never the scent of him.

Pup and Rex became a formidable team out foraging and stealing food from empty tables. Despite their size, they could slip through the shadows, unseen, and were strong enough to tip the biggest of bins. Lady Fifi's legs became so stiff that she hardly left her handbag on her mattress throne, although she was still quick to growl and grumble at them all. Saffy took Reynard on night food raids into people's back yards, but Reynard was always happiest in the dark shadows of the den where his fear of the Huntsman couldn't follow. Merle and Clown were fast-footed thieves: Merle the brains and Clown the joker in their double-act for survival.

And Frenchi was just Frenchi: brave, dependable Frenchi, with the weight of the world on his shoulders, licking his worry-paw in times of stress.

Pup now towered over Frenchi, but he still curled up next to his friend, pushing his head beneath Frenchi's paws to rest his head on Frenchi's chest and fall asleep to his soft rumbling snores.

As Pup grew older, he sometimes left the Railway Den by himself, loving the quiet nights when he could roam for hours, or the early dawns where he would watch the city wake up. His paws twitched with boredom as the days grew longer. He wanted to be out, exploring and running. His feet itched and twitched to be moving.

Frenchi groaned and grumbled when Pup went out by himself, but he understood that Pup needed to get out, to run, to learn about the world. He didn't want Pup to grow up scared like Reynard. He knew he had to trust Pup to stay safe, to keep to the rules, and that he had to learn by his own mistakes to survive.

But Pup hadn't been keeping to the rules. He couldn't help it. The first time he had broken the rules had been trotting across the park early one morning, passing a group of children. They were kicking a ball about on the grass when the ball had flown in his direction and rolled past his feet. He should have walked on and slipped into the shadows, but the children running towards him sparked a memory.

Pup nudged the ball towards them with his nose. He remembered doing this for his boy, and how his boy had come laughing and running after him. So Pup pushed the ball again, and ran with it towards the children. The children followed, kicking the ball between themselves and then to Pup. And Pup bounded and bounced between them all while they laughed and clapped. He wagged his tail when they called him Ronaldo. He sat with them while they shared their crisps and sandwiches. He was one of them, playing in the park, and it was the best feeling in the world.

Each morning the children came back and each time Pup would play football with them, charging after the ball. The children brought more food for Pup too: sausages, bread rolls and biscuits. After a game he would sit with them on the grass, tongue lolling out, letting the spring sunshine warm through his fur.

He didn't let any of the children touch him, except for one girl. She had crept closer with a bit of cheese on her outstretched hand. Pup had known that he should back away, but he couldn't. He let the girl run her hands along his head and through his fur, and he remembered the feeling when his boy had done the same. Gentle, kind hands touching him, and holding him. He closed his eyes and rested his head upon her knee.

'Good dog, Ronaldo,' she said. 'I wish I could take you home. I wish you could be mine.'

Pup rolled on his back for his tummy to be tickled, thumping his tail upon the ground.

'I'll come back tomorrow,' promised the girl, wrapping her arms around him and hugging him tightly.

'Uff!' barked Pup, watching her join the other children and leave the park. He wanted her arms around him again, to feel the shape of her.

He slipped away, back along the streets to the Railway Den. He knew he shouldn't be out in daylight. He hoped the others would be asleep and wouldn't notice him return. But when he crept through into the den, the other dogs were all sitting, waiting for him. He looked around them all and realized that Rex was missing.

'What's happened?' said Pup.

The dogs were silent for a moment, then the boards to the entrance of the Railway Den banged and Rex slipped through. He lay down next to Lady Fifi and watched Pup.

Lady Fifi rose to her feet and sniffed Pup.

Pup backed away from her. 'What is it?'

'Where have you been?' said Lady Fifi. She circled slowly around him.'

'Out,' said Pup. He tried to shrink away from her.

Lady Fifi came to a stop in front of him. She pushed her face close to his. 'Where? What were you doing?'

'Just out,' said Pup. He glanced around the other dogs, but they were all looking directly at him.

Frenchi walked up to him. 'Have you let yourself be seen?'

'No,' said Pup. But he couldn't meet Frenchi's eyes.

Rex growled softly. 'Tell the truth, Pup. We've all been worried where you have been going to. I followed you today. You have been in the park with young humans.'

Pup stared at his paws and whimpered. 'I couldn't help it.'

'Fool,' snapped Lady Fifi. 'You put us all at risk. You betrayed the pack.'

'I was just playing,' said Pup.

'And playing could cost us our lives,' she growled. 'Did you think of that?'

Pup backed away from them all towards the door. 'I'm sorry. Maybe I should leave you.'

'No,' said Saffy, walking up to him and wagging her tail. 'We want you here. You're safe here. Just stay with us and promise not to go to the park again.'

But Pup even shrank away from Saffy. 'I don't want to live like this, Saffy. I want to play with those children. I want to feel alive, not scared all the time.'

Frenchi turned to Lady Fifi. 'Surely young humans can't be much of a risk. Maybe we could let him join them now and again?'

'We can't risk being seen by Snatchers,' snapped Lady Fifi.

'Maybe it's safer if he's with them,' said Frenchi. 'Snatchers might think one of the children owns him.'

'We can't be seen,' said Lady Fifi.

'Then I must leave you,' said Pup. 'I can't put you at risk. And I can't live like this.'

Merle stood up and turned to Fifi. 'Clown and I let ourselves be seen at the markets,' she said. 'There's always a risk.'

'Merle's right,' said Clown. 'And Pup needs to have some fun. Surely we can let Pup live a little.'

'Don't let the Huntsman in,' whimpered Reynard.

'Shh!' said Saffy, licking Reynard's face. 'There are no huntsmen here.' She turned to Lady Fifi. 'Maybe one of us could go with Pup and stay in the shadows. We could look out for him while he plays.'

'I will do it,' said Rex. He walked out of the shadows

94

and looked Pup deep in the eyes. 'I've seen what this means to him.'

Lady Fifi growled and grumbled. 'It's a risk. But if you are all willing to take it, I won't stop you.'

'Thank you, Fifi,' said Frenchi. He nudged Pup. 'Come on. Let's get some sleep.'

'Thank you,' whispered Pup. 'All of you.'

Lady Fifi seemed to soften. 'I know what it's like,' she said. Her clouded eyes seemed to look far away into another lifetime. 'There was once a child that held me. My girl pushed me around and dressed me up in human clothes. She put this collar with jewels on me. She loved me. But the mother got bored of me, like she got bored of the handbags she carried.' Lady Fifi sighed. 'She left me in Dead Dog Alley in a handbag. I never got to say goodbye to my girl.'

'Oh, Fifi,' said Saffy. 'I'm sorry.'

But Lady Fifi was already on the way up to her mattress. She seemed smaller somehow. Older too. One small jewel in her threadbare collar caught the light and glinted in the darkness.

Pup stood beneath Lady Fifi's mattress. 'Lady Fifi, how long ago did you lose your girl?'

Lady Fifi curled into her handbag. 'A long, long time,' she said. 'I wasn't much older than you are now. Not long out of puppyhood.'

Pup sighed and lay down next to Frenchi. He closed his eyes and tried to sleep, but sleep wouldn't come. This was his life now, and maybe it would always be like this. Maybe he would be like Lady Fifi, growing old in a place that was damp and cold. He tried to think only about tomorrow when he could play with the children again and feel arms around him and forget for a brief moment that he was a street dog, without a human of his own.

Chapter 12
THE SEWER DOGS

Pᴜᴘ ᴡᴀꜱ ᴜᴘ ᴇᴀʀʟʏ ᴛʜᴇ next morning, leaving the Railway Den at dawn. He couldn't wait to play with the children again. Rex trotted alongside him to the park. The sky was hazy, promising sunshine as the day warmed up. A pale mist lay like a soft blanket across the lake.

'Let's wait under here,' said Rex, sliding beneath the low spreading branches of the rhododendron bush that Pup and Frenchi had sheltered beneath on Pup's first day as a street dog.

Pup joined him and lay down on the cool waxy leaves. His paws twitched in anticipation. He kept his eyes fixed on the wide spread of green grass in front of the lake where the children came to play football. A couple of joggers ran side by side together along the path, their strides matching each other. Then the swan lady came along, wheeling her trolley behind her. Pup watched the ducks and swans leave the safety of their island and glide across the water. They dabbled and gobbled the food she threw for them.

But Pup didn't go to see her. He was waiting for the children and knew they would be along as soon as the sun rose above the trees in the park. He chewed on a stick, stripping the bark and spitting the pieces on the ground. He watched a man walking a spaniel, throwing the ball for the dog to fetch. Pup glanced at Rex who was snoozing beside him. 'Have you ever had a human of your own?' he asked.

Rex opened one eye. 'There was a man who chained me and beat me,' he said. He shuddered. 'I have no wish to be near humans.'

Pup watched the spaniel bound up to the man for his ears to be stroked, before bounding away again. 'Some are good,' he said. 'Maybe there is a person for each of us.'

Rex closed his eye again. 'And who would want a dog like me?'

'If I were a human, I'd choose you,' said Pup.

Rex thumped his tail on the ground. 'Thank you, Pup, but I prefer you as a dog.' He stretched his paws and went back to sleep.

Pup sighed and put his head on his paws. He watched the man and the spaniel walk away and disappear from sight. He felt a pang of jealousy, wanting what that dog had; to have a human to play with him and care for him.

Pup waited and waited, and then he heard the sound he wanted to hear. Children's shrieks and laughter came across the park. Then Pup saw them, kicking the ball ahead of them.

'Here they come,' said Pup, sitting up.

Rex opened his eyes and watched the children lay out jumpers as goalposts.

Pup's tail wagged from side to side, sweeping the dry leaves beneath the bush. He saw the girl stop and throw bread for the ducks. 'That's her,' he woofed quietly.

The ducks squabbled for the bread as she joined the other children. She looked around as if she were looking for Pup.

'I'm going,' said Pup, getting to his feet.

Rex sat up. 'Wait!' he said.

Pup turned to look at Rex, but Rex was staring to the far end of the lake, trying to see through the thin veil of mist.

'Something's not right,' said Rex.

Pup peered over Rex's shoulders to see what he was looking at. 'There's nothing there.'

'Exactly,' said Rex. 'I've been watching the small birds pecking in the soil for worms, but they've gone now. They're up in the branches.'

'Can I go and play?' said Pup.

'Just wait,' said Rex. He got to his feet and sniffed the air, but they were upwind from the birds and he couldn't catch any unusual scents.

The children were kicking the ball between them, and Pup's muscles quivered, desperate to join them.

'There's nothing there,' said Pup.

'Lie down,' ordered Rex. 'Stay still.' He flattened himself on the ground and Pup did the same.

Pup followed Rex's gaze along the lake. A moorhen called an alarm as it scuttled across the water. Then five shapes came bounding out of the mist. Five dogs were running, their bodies arching and bending as their feet flew towards the swans and ducks at the water's edge. The leader was a huge white dog, followed closely by a skinny whippet and a small, scruffy terrier. A wolf-like dog and a large, muscled dog ran wide into the lake, to stop the ducks escaping into the deeper water.

'The Sewer Dogs!' said Rex. 'That's Fang at the front. He's vicious.'

The Sewer Dogs plunged into the ducks and swans that flapped around them in a blur of wing and feather. Spray shot in the air, catching the light, like shards of broken glass. Fang chased a small duck, grabbing its leg, and he swung it around while it quacked helplessly. Snarls and barks came from the other dogs as they leapt after the fleeing birds. The children screamed and huddled together on the patch of grass as other people in the park stopped to look.

From the other side of the lake, two humans were running towards the dogs.

'Snatchers!' said Rex, pressing himself further to the ground.

Pup peered through the leaves on the low branches and saw that one carried a long pole, and the other carried a rope. Fang saw them, but with a mouthful of duck he couldn't bark. He ran from them along the path, scattering two joggers in his way. The wolf-like dog and its large companion followed close behind. The whippet saw the Snatchers and spun around with a yelp of warning, dodging their outstretched hands. But the scruffy terrier hadn't noticed them, too intent on chasing the ducks. Pup watched as a rope fell over the dog's head, and it was hauled to the waiting hands. Pup shrank against Rex as the humans pulled a muzzle over the dog's mouth and held it by the scruff of its neck, while it twisted and turned under their grasp. He could hear it snarling and yelping as it tried to escape.

Pup stayed silent as the Snatchers carried the dog away. The people stopped watching and went on their way, and the children started playing football again. Only the girl who had held him looked around the park, for the dog she had named Ronaldo, the stray dog she had played with. But her Ronaldo was nowhere to be seen.

'You can't come back here,' said Rex.

'I know,' said Pup quietly. He stared after the girl, wishing he could feel her arms around him.

'Let's get back before the Snatchers return,' said Rex.

Pup followed Rex back to the den. He knew he could never go back to the park. He could never play football with the children again. It had been a fleeting moment of happiness. A glimpse into a world he couldn't be part of, and even that had now been taken from him.

He was a street dog now.

He had to be fearful of men.

Pup and Rex were both out of breath and panting as they entered the den.

Merle jumped up, circling them. 'What happened?'

'The Sewer Dogs were in the park,' Rex growled.

'Snatchers too,' said Pup. He winced at the memory of seeing the terrier hauled away. 'They caught one of the Sewer Dogs.'

Reynard shrunk into the shadows. 'Are the huntsmen here?'

'We'll have to lie low for a few days,' said Frenchi. 'If the Snatchers got you too, you'd never come back.'

'Where's Dogsdoom, Frenchi? What happens there?' said Pup.

'There's only one dog I know who's escaped from there,' said Frenchi.

'Who?' said Pup. He flumped down, his muscles suddenly feeling sore and tired.

'Me,' said a trilling voice from the top of the mattress. Lady Fifi had woken from one of her slumbers and stuck her head over the top. 'And I'm never going back there. I'd rather die.'

Pup pricked his ears up. 'What happens there?'

'You don't want to know,' said Fifi.

'He should know,' growled Rex. 'He has to know why we can't be seen.'

Lady Fifi clambered down and walked stiff circles around Pup. 'Dogsdoom is a place of wire and concrete, and dogs yowling for their freedom,' she said. 'I know. I escaped from there, a long time ago. I was small and slipped beneath the wire in a yard where the Snatchers let us have a run.'

'Dogs stay there for ever?' said Pup.

'Some do,' said Fifi. 'Some live there for their whole lives. Maybe my brother Roly is still there. He could have escaped with me, but he didn't. The lucky ones get chosen by humans to go into a new family.' Fifi shuddered. 'But some are not so lucky. A different fate awaits them.'

'What?' asked Pup.

'Enough,' said Frenchi. 'All you need to know is that if you go there, we can't find you again.'

'He should know,' said Rex again. 'Tell him, Fifi. Tell him what you told us. Tell him about the Door.'

'The Door?' said Pup.

Lady Fifi couldn't answer. She turned and climbed back up to her mattress.

Rex answered for her. 'If you're a biter or a danger to man, you go through the Door of No Return. And I'm a forbidden breed. There's no other choice for a dog like me.'

'What door?' asked Pup.

'A big metal door at the end of a corridor,' said Rex.

'What's beyond the door?' whimpered Pup, curling his tail between his legs.

'No one really knows,' said Rex. 'But all dogs fear it. Once a dog is taken through the Door, no dog ever comes back.'

Chapter 13
NIGHT PROWLERS

PUP DIDN'T VISIT THE PARK again, however much he wanted to. He changed his route each day to make sure the Snatchers wouldn't find him. He learned to use all his senses. He could spot a Snatcher from a distance. Most people didn't notice the street dogs. They were invisible to them. But the Snatchers watched the shadows, and their eyes followed Pup's moves. But Pup was too fast, too careful. He slept by day and used night-time to search for food and explore the city. Sometimes Pup and Frenchi would walk all night through the parks, raiding bins and sleeping under the stars. On other nights, he and Clown would play and race each other along the soft mud of the riverbank at low tide, scattering the gulls.

As the long warm summer gave way to the first chills of autumn, the nights shortened, and Pup could feel a thick undercoat begin to grow beneath his fur to keep him warm. His pads had hardened from walking the streets, and he knew every back alley and cut-through to escape. Sirius had returned to the night sky, rising in the southeast before dawn, and Pup would feel some comfort and protection under his watchful eye.

It had been a whole year since Frenchi had found him in Dead Dog Alley, and with that remembered cold night of autumn came the rain and wind again. It whirled down the alleyways and streets. The water ran down gutters and dripped from the ceiling in the den. The den was cold and damp and it was difficult to stay warm. Frenchi and Pup curled together to keep warm and Pup noticed Frenchi's breathing became deeper and more laboured. He huffed and puffed, and his nose was permanently crusty and sore.

Reynard became more agitated too as the nights drew in. All through the summer, he had seemed almost happy, sometimes sitting out in the warmth of the long evenings, turning his damaged face to the sun. Sometimes he had played chase with Pup and Clown through the alleyways. But the dark nights brought his old fears to the surface. He would crouch in the shadows of the den and keep his eye fixed on the entrance, fearing the Huntsman. When he slept, he whimpered and yelped in his dreams.

'Humans hunt for foxes in the autumn,' Saffy whispered to Pup. 'This time of year is the hardest for him. We just need to get him through the winter.'

Reynard looked up at the ceiling of the den as a train rumbled above. 'The Huntsman rides the iron mare,' he said. 'He's hunting the night prowlers. And he's hunting me.'

'There are no huntsmen here,' whispered Saffy. 'You're safe with me.'

Reynard shivered. 'They're coming for you and coming for me. The night prowlers know where to go. They know where to hide.'

'Hush, Reynard,' said Saffy. 'You're safe with us.'

'When the night prowlers come, we must go with them,' said Reynard. 'We must run deep to the ground. We must hide deep beneath the earth.'

Saffy licked his ears. 'Shh! This is the safe place, right here, with me.'

The autumn wind howled into November and stripped the leaves off the trees. Rainwater pooled through the entrance to the den, forcing Rex back from his guarding place in the shadows. Foraging trips for food were cut short by the cold. The musty scent of fox often drifted into the den as the night prowlers used the road below the railway arches as a cut-through to their own dens and hunting grounds.

One night, Pup and Frenchi returned from a trip along the back of restaurants, foraging for left-overs. Both dogs were cold and wet to the skin and Pup's paws were sore from the wet, gritty ground. The food they had found that night had been greasy and tasteless, and it had left Pup feeling hungry and sick. He longed for the summer nights and warm evenings sitting out unseen in parks and in the cool shadows alongside the river. Summer had been full of left-over food from barbecues, rich meat and bones. But winter was approaching in full force, bringing the first autumn storm. Tall tower blocks disappeared into low cloud and the dark sky glowed orange from reflected street lights. The wind whipped around corners and blew over bins and scattered paper and plastic into the air. Cars and commuters hurried home, keen to get out of the storm, and Pup and Frenchi hurried back to the den too. The wind was rising, and the clouds promised more rain.

Merle circled them when they arrived back at the den. 'One two, three, four, five, six, seven and me. All here. All here,' she said, circling them again.

Even Clown seemed subdued by the storm. He curled in his corner, his ears flattened against his head, and looked warily at the entrance where the loose board of wood banged back and forth in the wind.

Fifi looked down from her mattress throne. 'The sky is pressing low today. My bones feel it. This will be some storm. I have not felt its like for some time. There is worse yet to come. It is best to stay here until it passes.'

Pup curled up next to Frenchi, trying to ignore the loose board banging and the wind whistling and howling. Lightning flashed, projecting monster shadows in the den. And as thunder rolled around the sky, the dogs fell into restless and dreamless sleep.

'Reynard! Where's Reynard?'

Pup woke to Saffy's calls.

'He's gone,' said Saffy, spinning around. 'Reynard's gone. I didn't hear him go.'

The other dogs woke, and Rex sniffed all around the den. Merle stood by the entrance. 'He's gone this way. I can smell foxes have been this way too.'

'We have to find him,' said Saffy. 'He's following the foxes, but they won't protect him.'

Rex shook himself and looked out into the wild night. 'I'll go.'

'I'll come too,' said Merle and Clown together.

'He'll need me,' said Saffy. 'He'll only listen to me.'

'I'll come,' said Pup.

Frenchi huffed and puffed. His chest had become wheezy

with the damp and cold. 'I'll only slow you down. Tell him we need him. He's part of our pack.'

Lady Fifi put her head over the mattress, looking at them from her cloudy eyes, but she didn't say a thing. She just watched Rex, Pup, Saffy, Merle and Clown disappear out into the night.

The rain stung Pup's eyes, and he could feel cold water soak deep into his undercoat. He looked up and down the street. 'Which way did he go?'

Rex put his nose to the ground. 'He went this way, towards the river.'

The rain had washed away some of the scents, but Reynard's scent was mixed with the musty smell of fox, and the five dogs ran, their feet splashing through the puddles. It was late and only a few cars were about, their headlights reflecting off the wet roads. Soon they were running alongside the river. Pup caught glimpses of it between the railings. The river was full. It was high tide and the choppy water churned and slapped on the walls of the riverbank. Boats heaved on their moorings and jostled each other, and a few boats were out on the water, their port and starboard lights rising and dipping in the heavy swell.

Rex stopped abruptly. 'I've lost the scent.'

Pup circled and sniffed around the ground too. Reynard's scent trail came to a sudden end, as if he'd vanished into thin air. Pup looked around them. 'He can't have just disappeared.'

Saffy jumped up onto the wall and looked out across the river. 'There he is!' she cried.

The others joined her and stared out over the waves.

The scent of fox drifted across the water.

'Where is he?' said Merle.

'I saw him,' said Saffy. 'I'm sure I did.'

'He's there,' said Clown, pointing his nose towards the middle of the river.

Far out in the dark waters, Reynard's head bobbed above the choppy surf. He was being swirled away by the strong currents.

'Reynard!' barked Rex.

'Reynard!' called Saffy. 'Come back!'

But Reynard didn't seem to hear. His mind was elsewhere, his nose following the scent of the night prowlers that whipped away across the river.

Pup began running along the top of the wall, following Reynard, trying to keep pace with him. 'Reynard,' he barked. 'Come back. Come back to us.'

But the water was dark, and Reynard's head became a small dot, rising and dipping behind the waves.

A large barge chugged slowly upriver between Reynard and the riverbank, blocking him from view. It sent a large wake of frothy water that slopped and gurgled against the wall of the riverbank. Lightning flashed neon yellow across the sky, illuminating the city for a heartbeat.

Pup paced up and down, waiting for the barge to pass, to search for Reynard again.

'Reynard!' he cried again. 'Reynard, come back.' His bark was whipped away by the wind.

Whether Reynard heard it or not, Pup would never know.

When the barge had passed, Reynard was nowhere to be seen.

He had disappeared deep beneath the stormy waters.

And Reynard, the foxhound, was gone.

Chapter 14
A LAND OF GOLD

'REYNARD!' CRIED SAFFY.

She didn't stop. She leaped out from the riverbank, following Reynard.

Rex followed close behind and sprang after her, their bodies crashing into the water together. Saffy's head came up to the surface and she looked for Reynard but couldn't see beyond the choppy waves. She couldn't find the scent of him.

Rex swam to the other side of her, his paws pulling hard in the strong current. He pushed her back towards the riverbank. 'He's gone, Saffy. We can't reach him.'

Saffy tried to swim past Rex, but Rex kept pushing her back, and holding onto the loose scruff of her neck. Both dogs struggled, the water spinning and pulling them, but they reached the stone steps to the top of the riverbank. Merle, Clown and Pup raced down to them, helping to push Saffy up.

Saffy shook the water from her coat and looked out over the dark water. 'I should have heard him leave.'

Rex doubled over, coughing water. 'It's not your fault.'

'I loved him,' said Saffy. 'I loved him like my own pup.'

Clown and Merle joined them. 'Maybe Reynard is with the foxes,' said Clown. 'Maybe he's found them after all.'

'One less,' whispered Merle, counting in her head. 'One less.'

Pup stood a little way from the others, staring into the

dark water and feeling an empty Reynard-shaped hole in his heart. He threw back his head and he howled. He howled for Reynard. He howled for all the things he could not change or understand. He howled because it was the only thing he could do.

And for once, no one stopped him. The others raised their muzzles to the sky, threw back their heads, and they howled for Reynard too.

The dogs returned in silence to the den.

Frenchi watched as Saffy curled up in the corner with her back to the others. Rex lay down with a grunt and Merle and Clown paced by the entrance. The den seemed colder and darker. The walls oozed water and drips fell from the ceiling. A train rumbled overhead, the screech of steel brakes, a high-pitched scream.

Lady Fifi struggled down from her mattress. She wanted to be close to the others, feeling Reynard's loss too.

Frenchi coughed and spluttered and his chest wheezed. 'This place is no good for any of us. Fifi, isn't there somewhere else we can go?'

Fifi shook her head. 'We can't risk being seen. No one comes here.'

'Do we have to live here for ever?' asked Pup. 'For ever and ever?'

Frenchi sighed, and scratched his ear. 'The winters are the worst. It'll be better when summer comes again.'

'There must be someplace else where we can live,' said Pup. 'Where it's warm and dry.'

115

'We're street dogs,' Rex growled softly. 'We have no choice.'

Pup walked over to Saffy. 'You know a place, don't you?'

Saffy tucked her nose into her fur and kept her eyes closed, but Pup pawed at her.

'Saffy, you know a place. You said you once lived there, where you could run with the wind in your ears and the sun on your back. Why can't we go there?'

Saffy opened an eye. 'I'm not even sure if it is a real place,' she said. 'Maybe it is just in my dreams.'

'Or maybe it is real,' said Pup. 'What if it is? Please tell us about it.' He nudged her with his nose. 'What's it like, Saffy?'

Clown lay down at her feet. 'Please tell us, Saffy. Even if it isn't real, maybe we can escape there in our dreams too.'

Saffy shuffled to sit up, and her deep brown eyes seemed lost and faraway. 'There was a place I think I remember. I try to go there when the world seems too much. There's a beach of golden sand beneath blue-green hills. To get there, you must take a path through the sand dunes. You can smell the salt of the sea and hear the surf unfurling on the beach. As you rise up the last sand dune, you can see the whole sea spread out before you, and you run, and keep running out onto the beach, with the sun on your back and the wind in your ears, running and running and running along the beach. And when the sun slips down behind the sea, it turns the world to gold.'

'Where is this place?' asked Frenchi.

Saffy sighed. 'I don't know. All I remember is that it's a

place where the ocean meets the sky at the very end of the world.'

'How do we find it?' said Merle.

'I don't know,' said Saffy.

'If we follow the setting sun, it'll lead us there,' said Pup. 'We keep going until we reach the end of the world.'

'We don't know how far it is,' said Frenchi.

'It might not even be real,' said Rex.

'Then we must have faith,' said Pup. 'For tonight, Sirius will sink below the horizon where the sun falls sleeping. Maybe he is showing us the way.'

'I want to run on that beach, just run and run,' said Clown. 'And loop mad circles round and round where no one can stop me.'

'I want to run with you,' said Merle.

Saffy nodded. 'Maybe Pup is right. Maybe we have to have faith to find it.'

Frenchi stood up. 'What do you think, Fifi? Do you think we could try?'

Fifi turned her cloudy eyes to the entrance where the wind drove rain inside the den. 'Maybe there is a place far from here. It could be a long trek through the unknown,' she said. 'And I am too weak to travel far.'

'Then I will carry you in your handbag,' said Pup. 'We'll take you with us.'

Rex stood up from the shadows. 'And I will help carry you too.'

'No one gets left behind,' said Frenchi. 'We look after the pack.'

Lady Fifi was still for a moment. 'We will need to wait until the warmer days. It would be too dangerous to leave now.'

'When can we leave?' asked Pup.

Fifi turned and shuffled back up to her mattress. 'We will leave when the days stretch out, and when the trees wear their full coat of leaves.'

And so every day Pup thought of the place where the ocean meets the sky at the end of the world. He held onto hope and faith and looked up at the trees. Their bare branches were stark against the winter sky, but he could see the tiny buds, tightly curled, carrying a promised spring.

And it was all Pup could do to stare at them and will them into breaking into leaf.

The Boy

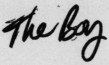

It is a cloudless night and the boy is looking up at the stars.

It is hard to see them beyond the orange haze of the city lights.

But they are there, shimmering in the dark winter sky.

It is cold, and his breath mists the air. He pulls his coat more tightly around him and stamps his feet to keep warm. He is searching for patterns of stars that will tell him the story about a hunter and his faithful dog.

He finds the three stars that make up the belt of Orion the hunter, and he follows them southeast to the constellation he is looking for. And there it is, Orion's hound, Canis Major, running beside him. One of those stars is brighter than the rest. It breaks through the city haze. It is Sirius, the dog star, shining from the great dog's heart.

And somehow the boy finds comfort in this.

He holds the small clay dog in his warm human hand, and he thinks about himself and Pup, and wonders if their story is written in the stars.

He lets himself dream that maybe Pup is looking up at these stars, wanting to find meaning in them too.

Chapter 15
RAMON

THE WINTER WAS COLD AND bitter. A freezing wind funnelled along the streets and the leaden skies brought endless driving rain. At night standing water froze to hard black ice. Pup was always glad to get back to the shelter of the Railway Den, where, although it was cold, it was sheltered from the wind and rain and never quite dropped below freezing.

'The Sewer Dogs are roaming further afield,' said Rex one night. 'I saw them along the riverbank looking for scraps.'

'I saw them too,' said Saffy. 'They tried to follow me, and I had to lose my scent in the river, then hide out for hours until they were gone.'

'Why would they follow us?' asked Pup.

Merle shuddered. 'Because they're looking for a new den. Theirs is easily flooded. I remember the winter I ran away from them.'

'You were a Sewer Dog?' said Pup.

'Not willingly,' said Merle. 'They found me and gave me protection, but it came at a cost.'

'We must be extra careful,' growled Lady Fifi. 'Don't take any chances.'

Clown was unusually quiet. He growled softly. 'We'll see them off, if they find us.'

Merle put her head in her paws. 'Fang is not a dog to be fought with. I saw him kill another dog.'

Pup looked up. 'He killed a dog? Why would he do that?'

'He was annoyed with it,' said Merle. 'It took his food. He rules by fear and rewards those who protect him.'

Rex prowled to the entrance of the den and looked out. 'It is not the way of a dog. Fang shames dogkind. He has learned the ways of humans, to be cruel and without care for another.'

Pup lay back down, but the thought of the Sewer Dogs unsettled him. The outside world felt less safe than before.

The sightings of the Sewer Dogs became more frequent. Pup stopped to watch them one day. They were on the other side of the riverbank and he was safely downwind. There were six of them. They were all big and powerful, except for the thin tail-tucked whippet he had seen the day they chased the swans in the park. They were scouring the low tide mud for scraps of food washed up on the shoreline. Pup noticed the other dogs in their pack cowered and put their tails between their legs when Fang faced them, and they squabbled amongst themselves for food behind Fang's back. Pup thought it was no wonder Merle had wanted to escape.

When Pup reported the Sewer Dogs on the riverbank, Lady Fifi restricted the foraging trips away from the river to the other side of the city.

'We don't want them to pick up our scent and follow it here,' she growled.

So Pup stayed well away from the river and didn't hear much about them for a while until Clown slipped into the den. He was agitated, pacing up and down. 'There's a Sewer

Dog that wants our help,' said Clown. 'I left him by the park, but he's injured.'

Saffy stood up. 'Then we must help him.'

'Leave him,' warned Rex. 'The other dogs might be near.'

'We can't leave him,' said Frenchi. He turned to Rex. 'For then we would become like the Sewer Dogs and not help each other.'

They all looked to Lady Fifi. She struggled to move from her mattress. 'It's too risky.'

'But you took me in,' said Merle. 'I'd be dead if it weren't for your kindness then.'

'We can't leave a dog in need,' said Saffy.

Lady Fifi shuffled to the entrance and looked out. 'All right,' she said. 'But Rex must go with Clown, to make sure the Sewer Dogs are not watching. Make sure you aren't followed.'

Pup waited in the den, pacing up and down. He didn't like the thought of another dog joining their pack. He slunk into the shadows when Rex and Clown led the thin whippet inside. The whippet looked even thinner than before. His bones showed through his skin, and he had a fresh wound on his face. His whole body shivered, and his tail was tucked low between his legs.

This time, Merle didn't rush out to circle and count the dogs. She remembered Ramon. He had arrived at the Sewers just before she made her escape. Ramon had the scent of the Sewer Dogs on him, and it filled her with remembered fear. She watched warily from the back of the den.

'Were you seen?' snapped Lady Fifi.

'No,' said Rex. 'We made sure we lost our scent walking through the lake, and I stayed back to check we weren't being followed.'

'Good,' she said. She clambered down from her mattress and circled the whippet who cowered even lower.

'Name!' barked Fifi.

'Ramon,' said the whippet. He licked his mouth and kept his head low. 'For the love of Lupus don't hurt me. Please spare me.'

Saffy stepped forward. 'No one's going to hurt you here.'

Fifi pushed past Saffy and glared at Ramon. She snarled, showing her one remaining canine tooth. 'Why were you outcast from the Sewer?'

Ramon carefully looked around him. 'There is not much food. I am smaller and weaker than the others and they fought me for food.' He pawed at the wound on his face.

'We can't feed another mouth either,' Fifi said.

'I can catch rats and mice. I'll hunt for you,' said Ramon. 'I'm faster than anyone.'

Rex circled him. 'Why have the Sewer Dogs been coming this way?'

'Looking for food,' said Ramon, trembling.

'Is Fang looking for us?' growled Rex.

Ramon stared at the ground. 'He's just looking for food.'

'You can't stay,' said Rex.

Ramon cast his eyes on Merle at the back. 'Hello again, Merle. You know what happens if the Sewer Dogs find me, don't you! Fang will kill me.'

Merle whined at the memory of the huge white dog.

'We can't cast him out,' said Saffy. She turned to Frenchi. 'You agree, don't you?'

Frenchi was unusually quiet. He walked to the entrance to the den and looked out, deep in thought. Then he turned back and sat with his face in the shadows. 'It would be wrong of us not to offer our protection.'

Lady Fifi climbed back up to her mattress, grumbling and groaning. 'He can stay, for now,' she said.

'Thank you,' said Ramon. 'May the love of the Great Sky Wolf protect you.'

Rex pressed his face next to Ramon's. 'You abide by our rules and you share your food. Is that understood?'

Ramon's tail curled further beneath him.

Saffy walked between Rex and Ramon and licked Ramon's sore face. 'You're safe here,' she said.

Merle lay down behind the protection of Clown.

But Rex paced up and down by the entrance, occasionally looking out in the night.

'What is it?' whispered Pup.

'Nothing,' said Rex. He watched Ramon from the shadows. 'Maybe nothing at all.'

Pup curled up with Frenchi like he always did and looked back at Ramon. The whippet had settled down, ready to sleep, but one eye was open, watching Rex. 'Frenchi,' whispered Pup, 'what if the Sewer Dogs do find us? What if they've followed our scent?'

Frenchi snuffled, trying to sleep. 'Rex was careful not to leave a trail, so sleep now.'

'But Frenchi . . . ?' whispered Pup.

But whether Frenchi had fallen asleep or was just pretending, Pup couldn't tell.

Rex sat sentry to the entrance of the den, sniffing the night air. Pup watched him for a long, long time, trying to stay awake until sleep finally came and stole him away.

Chapter 16
BETRAYAL

An uneasy silence fell over the Railway Den after Ramon's arrival.

Lady Fifi wouldn't let him out to go foraging for food the first few days, but when she did, she insisted that Rex accompany him. 'The Sewer Dogs might be near,' she said.

Ramon seemed constantly nervous. He sat watchful in the darkest corners of the den. He sought Saffy's comfort and stayed far from Rex. Pup felt a tension in the air. Maybe it had been the same when he had arrived at the den. Maybe it had taken time for the others to adjust to him being there and he hadn't noticed at the time.

Saffy mothered Ramon, giving him some of her share of food.

'He has enough to eat,' growled Rex. 'Save it for yourself.'

'You are too harsh on him,' said Saffy, licking Ramon's wounds. 'He has been through so much.'

Ramon nuzzled up against Saffy. 'May the great Sirius bless you for your kindness, Saffy,' he said.

Rex curled his lip and lay in the shadows. 'Sirius is no friend to us.'

'Sirius protects all dogs,' said Saffy. 'His is the brightest star.'

Rex growled softly and found a space in the furthest corner of the den.

Pup nestled down next to Frenchi, but the atmosphere in the Railway Den had changed. Rex seemed more distant somehow, quick to snarl and snap. When Rex left the den to go foraging for food, Ramon became less nervous around the others. He even played chasing games with Clown in the den, bouncing over the piles of rubbish and scattering paper into the air. Clown had found a dog faster than himself.

'We'll have to take Ramon to the night markets,' said Merle, joining in the fun.

Even Saffy seemed to relax when Rex was out.

When Rex stayed in the den, he kept himself away from the others. Frenchi tried to keep everyone happy, but Rex would grumble from the shadows.

Pup missed the old days in the den. He missed Reynard and he missed Rex's quiet companionship. He often went for walks by himself to look at the trees. Some of the buds were unfurling into leaf. 'When are we going to the golden place, Lady Fifi?'

Lady Fifi poked her nose out of her handbag bed. 'Not yet. A little later when the days are longer, and the nights are warmer.'

Ramon's ears pricked up. 'What is this place?'

'It is a place far from here,' said Clown. 'It is a place of long golden sand—'

'It's a safe place for us,' said Merle. 'A place we can be free.'

Ramon edged a little closer to them. 'It sounds like a paradise. Please tell me more about it.'

Lady Fifi interrupted with a soft growl. 'Enough, everyone. Sleep now.'

*

One evening, when Rex was out and Lady Fifi was snoring from her mattress, Ramon turned to the others. 'When are we leaving for the golden place?'

'When Fifi says we are ready,' said Clown.

'But Lady Fifi is nearly blind,' whispered Ramon. 'She is old and weak. How will she lead us? How do we know she even plans to leave this place?'

Clown glanced up at Lady Fifi's mattress throne. 'Maybe Ramon is right. Maybe she is just saying we will leave soon to keep us happy. Maybe she doesn't want to leave at all.'

'But she looks after us,' said Merle.

'Says who?' said Ramon.

Merle chewed on a split claw. 'Well, she says she keeps us safe.'

Ramon nodded. 'Exactly. Maybe she has you where she wants you. Maybe she is making sure you stay here to look after her.'

Merle looked up at Lady Fifi. 'Surely not,' she said.

'She always tells us what to do,' said Clown.

Ramon looked around them all. 'The Sewer Dogs all know there is a weak leader here. Have you seen Fang?'

Pup nodded, remembering the huge white dog.

'He'll take over this den,' said Ramon.

'What can we do?' said Merle. 'It's true Lady Fifi is too small to protect us against Fang.'

Saffy lifted her head. 'We trust her,' she said.

'Tell me, Saffy,' said Ramon, 'have you ever put too much trust in others and been let down?'

Saffy whined and put her head in her paws. She

remembered trusting the humans that stole her from the family she loved.

Frenchi got to his feet and stared Ramon in the eyes. 'Lady Fifi is our pack leader.' His words were sharp and said in a way to let everyone know that it was the end of the matter.

Ramon tucked his tail between his legs, and curled up next to Saffy, but Pup noticed Clown and Merle cast glances at Lady Fifi snoring in her bed. There was a seed of doubt where none had been before. Maybe Ramon was right? Maybe they needed a leader who could protect them from Fang? The pack felt weaker somehow and Pup began to wonder how he had never seen how vulnerable they were before.

The next night, when Rex took Ramon out to find food, Pup went with them. Rex took them far away from the river and the sewers.

Pup trotted alongside Ramon as they followed behind Rex. He kept thinking about what Ramon had said about Lady Fifi. 'Maybe Rex should be our leader,' Pup said. 'He's bigger than Fang.'

Ramon was silent for a moment, then he leaned close to Pup. 'Rex would be dangerous with that power. Have you seen the scars on him? He's a fighting dog.'

'Humans made him fight,' said Pup.

Ramon curled his lip. 'Dogs like him don't lose their instinct to kill. I wouldn't be surprised if he's attacked before.'

Pup kept silent, thinking about the time he saw Rex attack a person that first time he went foraging with him. He remembered how Rex had seemed possessed by a wild thing, unstoppable.

'You see,' confided Ramon. 'I can tell you know. You know what he is, don't you? He's a Forbidden. You can never trust a Forbidden.'

'I would trust Rex with my life,' said Pup.

'You are young, Pup,' said Ramon. 'Some dogs are not quite what they seem. Choose your friends wisely. Dogs like Rex have no love of Sirius. They do not honour the Great Sky Wolf or the sacred bond. Is that the company you wish to keep?'

Pup kept his head down and tried to untangle his thoughts. 'Rex would never harm one of us.'

Ramon gave Pup a sideways look. 'I hope he doesn't let you down. I've known dogs like him. You can never trust them in the end.'

Pup watched Rex that evening as they foraged for food. Could it be possible that Rex would attack any of them? Rex led them to a rubbish dump in a part of the city Pup had never been to before. Pup wrinkled his nose as they rummaged through cartons and plastic packaging. This place smelled of rotten food and stinking waste. A brown foul-smelling liquid oozed out from the mountain of trash. Pup didn't want to eat anything here.

They returned hungry to the den, and Pup curled up next to Frenchi. Clown and Merle had also been out and had been more successful. They had returned with a cardboard box with pieces of fried chicken. The smell of it filled the den. Lady Fifi clambered down from her mattress and took one, and Frenchi took another. There was one left.

Ramon looked across at Merle. 'You did better than us. Where did you go?'

'To the city centre,' she said. 'There's always lots of food chucked in alleyways.'

'Why didn't we go there?' said Ramon, casting a sly glance at Rex.

'Because there are too many people,' said Rex. 'I don't want to risk the chance of being seen.'

'Is that because of what you are?' said Ramon. There was the hint of a growl in his throat.

The other dogs stayed quiet but watchful. Pup glanced at Ramon and noticed that Ramon looked Rex directly in the eyes.

A dangerous silence filled the air.

'And what am I to you?' said Rex.

Ramon reached over and took the last piece of chicken. 'You're a Forbidden. And everyone knows Forbiddens can't be trusted by man or dog.'

Rex lunged at Ramon. He pressed him to the ground, snarling in his face.

Ramon whimpered beneath Rex's paws, dropping the piece of chicken from his mouth.

Saffy jumped up. 'Rex, let him go.'

Frenchi shuffled over. 'Come on, Rex, my friend. It's all right. Leave it now.'

Lady Fifi woke up and put her head over the top of the mattress. 'What's happening?'

Rex lifted his paw from Ramon and stared around them all.

Ramon got to his feet and found shelter behind Saffy. 'You see?' he said to the other dogs. 'I warned you. Once a biter, always a biter. None of us are safe.'

Rex said nothing. He took the last piece of chicken and slipped out into the night.

Pup stared after him, and Ramon came to stand beside him.

'I'm sorry,' said Ramon. 'You see, I had to challenge him to show you. A Forbidden can never truly be trusted in the end.'

Rex didn't return the next day or the day after that. Lady Fifi sent Ramon out to find food with Clown and Merle instead.

'Where's Rex?' said Pup to Frenchi as they curled together to sleep.

'I don't know,' snuffled Frenchi. 'I wish I did.'

'Is it true that Forbiddens can't be trusted?' said Pup.

Frenchi was silent and licked his worry-paw for a long time before he spoke. He turned to Pup. 'Trust your instincts, Pup. You're a street dog now. Always trust your instincts.'

Pup fell into a restless sleep where Ramon became a human Snatcher, with a dog's head and human hands, chasing Rex along dark alleyways that twisted and turned, trapping Rex in a maze, impossible to escape from.

Lady Fifi was concerned about Rex's absence too. She clambered down from her mattress throne and paced at the entrance. 'Has anyone seen him?'

'He's gone,' said Merle. 'One less. One less.'

'Oh, Rex,' said Saffy quietly. 'Where are you?'

Ramon curled up next to her. 'You are too trusting, Saffy,' he said. 'We are safer without him.'

Saffy moved away from Ramon and sat with Lady Fifi, looking out into the night. 'Yes,' she whispered. 'I think I have been too trusting. But I fear my misplaced trust has put us all in danger.'

That night Pup went with Frenchi to the bins at the back of the closest shop. Frenchi huffed and puffed all the way and Pup had to slow down for him to keep up. There wasn't much to pick out from the bins; some bread and some carrots that were old and chewy.

They returned to the den as dawn was breaking, but as they were curling up to sleep, Clown and Merle galloped into the den. They were both panting and wide-eyed.

Pup sat up. 'What is it?'

'Ramon has gone,' said Clown. 'He slipped away from us. I chased him, but I couldn't keep up.'

Lady Fifi growled from her mattress. 'Which way did he go?'

Merle trembled, her tail between her legs. 'He was heading across the river.'

'To the Sewers!' whispered Saffy.

'Why would he do that?' asked Pup.

Frenchi huffed and puffed to the entrance of the den. 'I think Ramon may have taken advantage of our kindness.'

'But why would he go back to the Sewer Dogs if he risks being killed?' asked Pup.

A growl came from Frenchi's throat. 'I think we're about to find out.' He took a step back into the den. 'The Sewer Dogs are coming down our street!'

Chapter 17
LADY FIFI'S LAST STAND

Pup LEAPED UP AND LOOKED out of the den too. In the pale dawn light, six dogs were walking shoulder to shoulder behind Ramon who was leading the way. Pup saw the size of Fang and shuddered. 'I wish Rex was here. Where is he?'

'I don't know,' said Frenchi. 'But this is exactly what Ramon wanted. To get Rex out of the way.'

'Go back inside the den,' said Pup. 'I'll stand guard.'

'I'll stand with you,' said Clown.

Lady Fifi scrambled down from her mattress. 'We'll fight them,' she said. 'We'll fight them to the very end.'

Frenchi looked back at her. 'We'll never win. Look at us. Maybe we should just let them have the den.'

Merle backed away into the shadows. 'If they find me, they'll kill me. I ran from them and they said they'd kill traitors.'

Pup put himself in the entrance, and felt his hackles rise up. His heart thumped inside his chest, and he wanted to tuck his tail between his legs and run, but he stood firm, his head and tail raised. 'What do you want?'

'To have your den, of course,' said Fang. 'Ramon here kindly led us to it.'

'This belongs to the Railway Pack,' said Pup. 'I can't let you in.'

Fang took another step towards Pup and bared his teeth. 'Your fighting dog isn't here. Ramon saw to that.'

Pup said nothing but growled.

140

'If you just let me in to talk to your pack leader, maybe we could come up with a deal,' said Fang. 'A compromise.'

Pup heard scuffling behind him, and Frenchi appeared. 'Lady Fifi says that just Fang can come in – with Ramon – but no more.'

Fang agreed. 'Stay here,' he growled to the other dogs. 'Only come if I call.'

Fang and Ramon slipped through into the gloom. Pup slid back to let them pass, meeting Fang's stare as he came inside. Fang was shorter than Pup at the shoulder, but he was stocky and muscled. His head was broad, and his ears ripped and scarred. He looked like a dog that had seen many fights. Pup and Clown placed themselves by the entrance again and watched Fang stop in front of Lady Fifi.

Fang looked around. 'Nice place,' he said. 'Warm. Dry. Plenty of space.'

Saffy stepped forward. 'Why did you do it, Ramon?' she whispered. 'Why did you go back to him? We took you in. We could have protected you.'

Ramon said nothing but couldn't look Saffy in the eye.

Fang turned round to face her. 'Because Ramon saw sense. He knows that we would find you eventually. And if we found you, we wouldn't spare him.' He looked around the den and saw Merle in the shadows. 'Hiding again, are you, Merle? Ramon said you were here.'

Fifi stepped in front of Fang. 'Leave this place and leave us,' she growled. She stood defiant in front of him.

Fang turned his attention to Lady Fifi. He bent his head down, his immense size shadowing her. His head was

141

bigger than her body. 'I'll do a deal. Your pack can stay, but I become the new leader.'

Pup watched Fifi, and for the first time he saw her falter. Her eyes darted about and her tail tucked between her legs.

Long strings of saliva dripped from Fang's mouth onto her head.

'You are right,' said Fifi. 'You are bigger and stronger than us. We will leave. This den is yours.'

'That's not what I said,' growled Fang. 'I said I will be the leader, and then when the spring comes, you will show me the way to the secret place.'

'There is no secret place,' said Fifi.

Fang growled. 'I know there is. Ramon told us about your plans, and you will take us to the place of the long golden sand.'

Fifi stepped back. 'We don't even know where to find it.'

'You expect me to believe that?' snarled Fang. 'Now, as I've said, your pack can join ours and do as I say. All except the collie. Her fate was sealed the day she left us.'

Merle whimpered from the corner, and Frenchi and Saffy stood protectively in front of her.

Fifi's whole body trembled. She held her head up high. 'This is my pack. These are my dogs. I will protect them to the last.'

'Stand aside,' said Fang.

'No,' said Fifi.

Fang was swift and brutal. In one single movement he snatched Fifi in his jaws and shook her like a rat. Lady Fifi snarled and yelped, her last peg-like rotten teeth and gums clamping on the folds of his lip. Then he flung her small body to the floor.

Lady Fifi tried to stand, but her legs gave way beneath her, and she lay, her chest rising and falling as she strained for breath. 'Get out,' she spluttered. 'Get out of my den.'

Fang turned to the others. 'I'm your leader now. But first, I'll deal with the collie.'

Frenchi and Saffy backed away, still shielding Merle.

Pup bent his head to Clown. 'Guard the entrance – they can only fight you one at a time. I'll take on Fang.'

Fang approached Frenchi and Saffy. 'Futile bravery,' he said. 'An old lame Labrador and a fat French bulldog. Get out of my way. If you defy me, I will kill you too.'

'You'll have to kill me first,' said Pup, stepping in front of Fang.

Fang paused and looked him up and down. 'It'd be a shame to kill you. A big dog like you could join us.'

'Never,' growled Pup.

'You are no match for me,' snarled Fang. 'You are barely out of pup-hood. Run, while you can, little dog.'

Pup curled his lips, showing his row of sharp white teeth. 'No. This is my pack.'

The hackles on Fang's back raised up, making him look even bigger. He took a step towards Pup. 'Get out of my way.'

Pup growled and stared back at Fang. He looked him right in the eyes. 'You'll have to make me.'

Pup wasn't prepared for the speed of Fang.

Fang lunged forward and Pup felt himself pinned to the ground while Fang's jaws clamped down on his head and neck. Pup squirmed and kicked him with his back legs, managing to free himself, but Fang was faster and flipped him over. Frenchi and Saffy joined in, followed by Merle who bit at Fang's tail and legs. Fang's attack on Pup was savage, never letting up for a moment. He was a fury of teeth. Pup was fighting for his life. All he could hear was the snarling from Fang's throat.

He didn't hear the barks and growls from outside the den, or see the blur of a shadow storm into the den.

Rex had returned.

He launched straight at Fang, ramming his head into the large dog's belly. Fang fell and gasped for air but Rex was on him, biting and gouging at him with his claws and teeth. When Fang tried to get up, Rex forced him down, ripping at his ears and tearing his skin. The other Sewer Dogs fought their way past Clown, but Pup, Clown and Merle fought them back.

Rex battled Fang into a corner and paused for a moment. 'Call your pack off and leave.'

Fang's tail was between his legs and his eyes darted about.

'Call them off,' growled Rex, blood and saliva dripping from his mouth. 'Or I will kill you.'

Fang snarled, his head low. Blood poured down the side of his face, bright against his white fur. 'Get outside,' he called to the Sewer Dogs. He turned to Rex as he left. 'We'll be back.'

Ramon whimpered, staying just inside the entrance.

'You too,' barked Rex. 'Get out. You led them here.'

In the silence that followed, Pup limped over to Lady

Fifi with the others. They formed a circle around her. All the dogs had been badly bitten. Some wounds were deep into their flesh. But Lady Fifi was broken, and struggling to breathe.

She lifted her head. 'You came back, Rex.'

Rex lay down beside her. 'I never left. I knew Ramon was up to something. I could see he was trying to turn us against each other. I've been watching the Sewer Den for days. But when I found them gone this morning, I guessed they had come here. I just wish I'd got here sooner.'

'You saved us,' she said.

Rex looked at the others, bitten and bruised. 'We did it together.'

Saffy licked Lady Fifi's wounds. 'Rest now, Fifi,' she said.

Lady Fifi struggled to speak between breaths. 'Find that place,' she rasped. 'The place where the ocean meets the sky at the end of the world.'

Pup nudged Fifi with his nose. 'We're taking you with us, remember.'

Lady Fifi closed her eyes. 'I hear the Great Sky Wolf calling me.'

'Stay with us, Fifi,' said Clown.

Frenchi shuffled forward and curled around Fifi, trying to keep her warm, but she felt cold to touch.

'He's coming,' murmured Lady Fifi. 'I see him.'

'Safe journey, dear friend,' Saffy whispered. 'Find Reynard and run as sky wolves together.'

The tip of Lady Fifi's tail twitched. One last breath ruffled the long strands of fur around her nose, and then she was still.

Merle limped a circle round them all and stopped at Lady Fifi's broken body. 'One less,' she said. 'One less.'

'She never got to come with us to the place where the ocean meets the sky,' said Pup.

Rex looked to the entrance of the den. 'We must leave as soon as possible,' he said. 'When our wounds have healed, and we are all fit to travel, we will do as Lady Fifi asked, and we will go. For the Sewer Dogs will return. I am not afraid of them, but I fear that they will draw attention to us in the eyes of man.'

Saffy pawed at Lady Fifi's broken body. 'She was wise and brave. She gave her life for us.'

Frenchi nodded. 'She was a true leader. She kept us safe for so long.'

'Come,' said Rex to the others. He picked up Fifi's small body in his mouth and led the way out of the den to the river, where he set her body down on the soft mud at the water's edge.

Pup sat with the others in the cool blue shadows of dawn. The stars began to fade in the brightening sky. Together, they watched the creeping tide slip beneath the brave Lady Fifi. The water curled gently around her, lifted her up and carried her away.

Chapter 18
SNATCHERS

PUP'S WOUNDS SLOWLY HEALED. IT took a few weeks before he could walk without a limp. The broken skin on his neck formed a tough scar.

Merle was restless, circling the other dogs, counting and re-counting the dogs in her pack. But two of her flock were missing, and she couldn't herd them back again. It gnawed and gnawed at her collie soul. Reynard was gone, and now Fifi. *Two less, two less, two less*, she whispered in the dark hours.

The nights were still cold, and the days were interrupted by sharp, sleety showers, but the dogs picked up on Merle's restlessness.

Saffy nodded. 'I think it's time we left. I keep thinking about the beach of white sand.'

Clown bounded about, chasing a bee that had bumbled into the den. 'Me too. I imagine a place where you can run, and not stop running.'

'I don't feel safe here any more,' said Merle.

'Me neither,' said Saffy.

'When can we leave?' asked Pup.

Frenchi shuffled to the entrance to the den and looked up at the clear blue sky. 'We'll leave tonight, when darkness falls and the dog star, Sirius, can show us the way. We'll follow him home.'

Rex sighed. 'Home,' he repeated. He joined Frenchi and looked up at the sky. 'Maybe there is such a place for us.

Just for dogs. No humans. Somewhere safe and warm with plenty to eat.'

'Let's rest,' said Frenchi, 'and save our energy for our escape tonight.'

Pup curled up and watched the shaft of sunlight that sliced through into the den turn with the arc of the sun. His thoughts were filled with Fifi and Reynard. If they weren't in this world any more, then where could they be? 'Who are the sky wolves?' he whispered.

Frenchi opened one eye. 'Some say they are our wolf ancestors who welcome us home when we die.'

Rex stretched out in the darkness. 'Only in death can we be truly free of man.'

Saffy yawned and settled into sleep. 'Some say they are our wild souls set free to run together with our pack.'

'This is our pack,' said Pup.

Frenchi gave Pup's nose a lick. 'And soon we will be able to run free together across the sand with the wind in our ears and the sun on our backs.'

Merle circled them all again. 'Sleep now,' she said. 'For tonight our new life begins.'

There was anticipation in the air. Even Rex seemed changed. He was silent and watchful, but a strange calm came over him. Pup's paws twitched with the promise of a journey. They would be following Sirius, the dog star, to the place where the ocean meets the sky at the very end of the world.

It had been real in his dreams for so long now.

And Pup couldn't wait to set out.

*

Maybe if they had set out before dark, they would have got away.

But the presence of the Sewer Dogs had brought the Snatchers close. People had seen large dogs entering the derelict archway and heard dogs fighting each other. The Snatchers had been called to deal with large and dangerous dogs roaming the streets.

Pup was the first to be aware of them. Their scent drifted into the den on the breeze. It brought the remembered panic of seeing one of the Sewer Dogs captured in the park.

Pup peered out. A van was parked further down the road and two men climbed out and rummaged in the back.

'Snatchers!' he barked loudly.

The other dogs jumped to their feet. The den was no place to be caught and cornered.

Rex looked up and down the street. 'Out, now! Everyone. Let's scatter and meet by the riverbank.'

The men were walking their way, carrying ropes and a pole with a loop at the end.

'Run!' yelped Frenchi.

Clown stuck with Merle and they galloped fast and furious right past the Snatchers. Clown did a loop right around them and then spun away, following Merle. There was no way the Snatchers with their two legs could keep up.

Frenchi made use of their distraction, shuffling as fast as he could down the opposite alleyway. The shadows swallowed him up and all that could be heard were the clicking of his nails on the concrete and his huffing and puffing fading into the distance.

Pup bounded away from them all towards the street and

the train station. He turned to look back, but saw that Saffy had tried to run past the Snatchers too. But Saffy was too slow on her old stiff legs. One man sprinted towards her and dived, pulling her down. She yelped as she hit the ground, a cry of pain and fear.

Pup didn't think twice. He turned back and ran, barking at the men as they tried to grab him too.

'Don't bite them,' yelped Saffy. 'Remember, don't bite.'

Pup jumped up and pushed at the men but felt himself jerked backwards as a rope came over his neck and pulled him to the ground. He clawed at it as it pulled tighter, choking his breath, and into the chaos came Rex, lips curled back, trying to sink his teeth into the Snatchers. But somehow, they evaded him. One tightened a rope around him. He twisted and turned to get away, snarling and growling, but he couldn't escape. In the blur, Pup could see the man tie rope around Rex's muzzle and wrestle him down.

Pup felt himself lifted up and bundled into a wire cage in the back of the van with Rex and Saffy. The doors slammed shut and plunged them into darkness.

He had let himself be caught.

The dream of following the dog star to the end of the world had gone.

Pup threw back his head and he howled.

He howled for the lost dream.

He howled for his friend Frenchi.

He howled because he didn't know if he would see him again.

He howled because he never said goodbye.

Chapter 19
DOGSDOOM

'HUSH NOW,' SAID SAFFY, LICKING Pup's face.

'They're taking us to Dogsdoom,' said Pup. Light seeped in through the gaps in the van doors and his eyes adjusted to the darkness.

Rex had pressed himself into the far corner, and clawed at the rope around his muzzle, but he couldn't remove it. Pup tried to help, but Rex thrashed and growled at Pup too.

'Saffy, I'm scared,' whimpered Pup.

'Remember the bond between us and people,' said Saffy. 'Don't bite. Be their friend.'

Saffy's voice sounded soothing and calm, but Pup could feel her whole body trembling. They lay in silence after that, close together, feeling the sway and turns of the van as it took them far from Frenchi, Clown and Merle, and towards Dogsdoom.

Pup didn't know what to expect from Dogsdoom. But what hit him first was the noise. He could hear it before the van slowed down to a stop. Howls and yelps and barks seemed to come from all sides. There were voices calling out for attention, for food, to be left alone and to be played with. There were angry voices, bored voices but mostly lonely voices, calling out to be heard. The van doors swung open and Pup could see they were in a large central courtyard surrounded by high grey walls. The smell of Dogsdoom was not only of dog but also a chemical stench that stung Pup's nose. There were human scents too. All these scents and noises were mixed up together.

Pup was hauled out of the van and separated from Rex and Saffy. A lead was slipped over his head and he was led into a bright room where someone pushed and prodded him. They looked into his ears and mouth, and ran their hands all over him, and even stuck something up his bottom. Finally, he had a small chalky white pill pushed into his throat and he was forced to swallow. He was sprayed with a liquid that made him cough, then he was led back through the courtyard into the grey kennel buildings. There were rows and rows of kennels. Each kennel had a concrete floor and steel bars that separated it from its neighbour. Dogs of all shapes and sizes looked at him from their kennels. Some cowered at the back, some wagged their tails, and some flung themselves at the bars, growling and snarling at him. Pup kept close to the human leading him, until he was put into an empty kennel.

'Good dog,' the woman said. She slipped the lead from him and left, shutting the kennel door. The bolt scraped across, and the woman crouched down and looked in. 'Be a good boy. Let's hope you don't stay too long.'

Pup stared at the woman as she left and watched her walk away. He turned around and paced the concrete floor between the bars. There was a soft bed in the corner of the kennel and a bowl of water. Pup looked for a window to look at the sky, but there was no window. Only a strip of harsh white light lit the kennels.

'Pup, is that you?'

155

Pup spun round. 'Saffy!'

Pup hadn't noticed Saffy in the confusion of noise and scents of other dogs. She was in the next kennel. Pup pressed himself against the bars to be close to her. 'Where's Rex?'

'I don't know,' said Saffy.

Pup paced a circle in his kennel. He scrabbled at the concrete floor with his claws, but made no mark on it. 'I don't like it here, Saffy. I can't get out. I can't see the sky.'

Saffy said nothing.

There were more footsteps and two people were walking down the corridor between the kennels carrying a long stretcher between them. Pup watched as they set the stretcher down by the kennel next to Saffy. Pup could see a large dog. He could smell Rex mixed with other human smells.

'Rex!' Pup barked. 'Is that you?'

The dog's ear twitched but he looked quite still and asleep.

'Rex?'

The people rolled the dog off the stretcher and onto a soft bed. They took off the muzzle from around his nose and backed out of the kennel, sliding the bolt across.

'It is Rex,' said Saffy, peering out of her kennel. 'He's asleep.'

'Rex!' barked Pup.

But Rex didn't move. He lay on the ground, his ear twitching as if he were listening.

'Rex! Wake up,' barked Pup again.

Rex lifted his head, his tongue lolling out to the side, then his head dropped down to the ground again.

'What's wrong with him?' whimpered Pup.

'I think he is asleep,' said Saffy.

'He's drugged,' said another voice.

Pup looked across to the kennels opposite him to see a dog staring at him. It was a small dog, with wiry hair and white bushy eyebrows. Its canine teeth stuck out at angles. It looked familiar.

'Is he a biter?' said the dog.

Pup didn't say anything.

The dog stood on his hind legs to get a better view of Rex. 'Is he . . . ?' He stopped then took a back-step. 'Is he a Forbidden?'

'None of your business,' said Pup.

'He must be,' said the dog. 'The Needles drug the forbidden breeds and biters to examine them, de-flea and de-worm them. Got to get the little hoppers off before you get put in here.'

The dog looked old. Very old.

'How long have you been here?' asked Saffy.

'For ever and a day,' said the dog.

Pup felt as if the walls were closing in. 'How do we get out?'

The dog studied them for a moment. 'Well, I don't rate your chances, any of you.' He turned to Saffy. 'No offence, love, but you're old. Too old to love.' He sniffed. 'You smell a bit too, dear, though no doubt the Aprons can sort out your ears.'

Saffy huffed and grumbled and turned her back on him, but Pup couldn't help staring.

157

'And you,' said the dog, looking Pup up and down. 'Well, I don't fancy your chances either. Too big for a start. You've gone past cute and cuddly. You've got a guard dog look about you. Not many want something like you, and the Aprons are careful who they give dogs like you to. Not all Lookers want to give you a good home.'

Pup just stared at him. The dog's words, like Aprons, Needles and Lookers, were swirling in his brain. 'Who are Aprons, who are the Lookers?' he asked.

The dog sat down, clearly enjoying having an audience. 'Aprons are the people here who feed us, bath us, walk us and train us. They're good, most of them. Avoid Swift-Kick Mandy though. The Needles poke sharp things into us, but make us feel better when we're sick. The Lookers come and look at us, and some take us away and give us a real home.' He glanced across at Rex. 'Don't fancy his chances at all,' he whispered. 'Forbidden breeds go to . . . well, I'd better not say.'

'They go through the Door,' whispered Pup. 'We know about the Door.'

The dog gave him a curious look. 'Where did you hear that?'

'Someone told me,' said Pup. 'A dog that escaped from Dogsdoom.'

The dog gave him an even more curious look. 'There's been only one dog to escape from Dogsdoom.'

'Just the one?' asked Pup.

'Yes,' said the dog. 'The only dog to escape was my sister.'

'Lady Fifi?' said Pup. He looked at the small, scruffy

158

terrier with wonky teeth and could see the resemblance. 'Then you must be Roly.'

The dog puffed his chest out. 'Lord Roland, Tunnock's Wafer, Archibald the fifth, of Tunbridge Wells, to you,' said Roly. 'And I was the first born in the litter.'

Pup just stared at him.

'Well, this is a surprise,' said Roly. 'How is my sister? How is the old girl?'

Pup glanced at Saffy. 'Fifi died,' he said. 'I'm sorry.'

Roly paused for a moment, then snorted. 'Ha! I won. I lived longer. I said I would. I told her life was better in here.'

Saffy turned to look at him. 'Fifi was a free dog. She answered to no one.'

'There's no such thing as a free dog,' said Roly. 'Always hungry, always on the run. Living in fear of hunger, being caught, being cold. What life is that? I said to Fifi before she escaped, I said it can't get much better than this. It's warm, it's dry, plenty of food. The Aprons treat you well, as long as you do what they say.'

'What if you don't?' said Pup.

'Then you go where he's going,' said Roly, looking at Rex and not trying to keep his voice down. 'If you don't honour the bond between man and dog, you go through the Door of No Return.'

'Shut up,' said Saffy.

'It's true,' said Roly. 'It's always the same with the biters and the Forbiddens. At the end of the day, after the Lookers have been and while other dogs are having their exercise in the open runs, the Needles come and take the biters away. They fold up their blankets, as if they'd never existed.'

Saffy curled her lips in a snarl that Pup had never seen on her before. 'Just shut up.'

Roly growled back at her. 'You should put your teeth away too. An old mutt like you, with bad breath and stinky ears. Haven't you heard of the bond between man and dog? We are their servants.'

'We are not their servants,' she growled. 'We are their friends. We are their guides.'

Roly stared at her. 'Think what you like. The truth is, you're in Dogsdoom now. And for an old dog like you, you're in here for life. There's no other way out.'

Chapter 20
SMALL
RED FOX

AFTER FIVE NIGHTS IN DOGSDOOM, Pup had learned the routine. The quiet of the early morning was broken by the sound of the Aprons unlocking doors. The howls and barks rose up calling for food, for attention, to be heard. Pup couldn't help joining in too; he threw back his head and barked, his voice rising above the others.

The Aprons would feed them, then let them go to the outside runs for exercise while they cleaned the kennels, hosing the floors and sloshing over liquid with the sharp scent that stung his eyes and obliterated all other smells.

Rex hadn't spoken to Pup or Saffy since they had been in Dogsdoom. When the Aprons came he growled and wouldn't let anyone touch him. They had to drag him out with a rope and a pole to clean his kennel. Then he curled back up again in his corner, as if he were trying to curl up so small that he might disappear. Pup tried to get him to talk to him, but Rex had turned his back on the world and refused all food.

The only thing Pup had to look forward to were the training sessions when the Aprons took him out into the yard to teach him how to sit and stay, how to walk to heel and how to fetch a ball. Pup loved it and he could tell the Aprons loved training him too. They called him Buster and he was quick to learn the new name they gave him. He learned their commands quickly too. Sometimes he became too bouncy and too quick. He didn't realize his own size and sometimes

162

knocked them over. He was strong and loved the reward game of tug-of-war, pulling the Aprons around. It was better than being stuck in the kennel all day. He loved it when they patted him and tickled his tummy.

Saffy didn't have any training sessions. Maybe she was too old for training, Pup thought. Instead, the Aprons and the Needles all loved to sit beside Saffy and give her cuddles. And she mothered them too, like she mothered all things. After Pup's training it was back in the kennel all day, then a quick evening walk around the courtyard. After supper, the lights were put out. Pup tried to tell himself the story of Sirius to bring him some comfort. But it was only when night came that Pup realized he missed seeing the stars.

Despite knowing the routine, Pup couldn't stop pacing. He paced up and down. Up and down. He couldn't keep still. His legs cried out to move. He walked seven steps to the end of his kennel, spun around, walked back seven steps, spun around again, and again and again.

'Oi!' yapped Roly one morning from his kennel. 'Pack it in, would you? You're making me exhausted just watching you.'

'There must be a way out if Fifi found one,' said Pup.

'There isn't now,' said Roly. 'She escaped under the wire of one of the runs. Now all the wire is fixed in the concrete.'

Pup paced up and down again.

'I said, give it a rest,' yapped Roly.

Saffy growled softly at him. 'Turn the other way and let him be.'

'Oh, put your manky teeth away, you old fleabag,' grumbled Roly. 'Besides, if he paces like that, he'll wear his pads out and they'll be raw and bleeding. I've seen it happen to other dogs.'

Saffy glanced at Pup. 'Hey,' she said gently. 'Why don't we see if Rex is ready to talk?'

Pup paced to the wire and pressed his head against it, looking at Rex who was curled with his back away from them.

'Rex?' said Saffy softly. 'Rex. Are you all right?'

Rex said nothing.

'Please answer,' whimpered Pup. 'We need you. I need you.'

Rex's ears twitched, and after what seemed a long time he lifted his head to look at Pup. 'I can't help you in here, Pup,' he said. 'I can't get you out. I can't defend you. I'm nothing here.'

'We both need you,' whispered Saffy.

But Rex turned his back and pushed his nose into his tail and closed his eyes again. 'You know what happens to dogs like me.'

Pup whined. 'Don't say that, Rex. Maybe it's not true.'

'Hey-up!' yapped Roly to the whole kennel ward. 'It's time, it's time, it's time. The Lookers are coming. Sit up straight. Look smart. Today might be the day.'

'The Lookers?' said Pup.

'The Lookers come for two days out of every seven,' said Roly. 'The Lookers choose dogs to take home. Today might be the day,' yapped Roly again, whipping the other dogs into a frenzy.

'Today might be the day,' barked a small terrier. 'Today might be the day.'

'Today's the day,' barked the other dogs. 'Today's the day.'

Pup watched the other dogs as the sounds of human voices drifted down the kennels. Bolts were being drawn back, and doors clanged open and shut. Pup noticed some dogs did as Roly said. They sat up, paws together, head tilted to the side in the way humans seemed to like. Other dogs just turned their backs as if they'd seen it all before.

'How many dogs get chosen?' asked Pup.

'Depends,' said Roly. 'Sometimes none, sometimes several will be chosen. You can't tell until the day. But I know if someone will be chosen.'

'How?' said Pup.

'Sometimes there's The Look,' said Roly.

'The Look?'

Roly strutted up and down authoritatively. 'With some dogs and humans, there's a moment. A really brief moment where human and dog look at each other and just know they have to be together.'

'How can you tell?' asked Pup.

'You'll know,' said Roly. 'There's nothing else like it.'

Pup glanced at Rex whose back was turned, but Pup wanted to see these humans. He remembered his boy's hands stroking his ears, and his arms around him. Maybe there could be another human he could love. He sat at the front of his kennel, feet together, his tail ready to wag.

Saffy saw him. 'Well done, Pup.' She did the same too, hobbling to the front of the kennel, waiting for the humans with her big brown eyes. Once, long ago, her big brown eyes had melted human hearts. Maybe they could again.

'Fleabag,' muttered Roly. 'Stinky smelly old dogs don't get chosen.' He snorted, chuckling to himself.

Saffy turned away to the back of the kennel. It was true. She was old. Her ears itched, and brown gunge often came out when she shook her head. She was stiff too and she couldn't play ball any more. Roly's words had cut into her.

'Shut up, Roly,' growled Pup. 'Any human would be lucky to have Saffy as a friend.'

Roly was enjoying the reaction from Pup. Life was boring enough in Dogsdoom, so it was fun to have an argument. 'Thing is,' said Roly, his scruffy hackles rising, 'it's not us who do the choosing. It's them. The humans. And I can't think of any reason why a human would choose a smelly, hairy old dog with bad breath, can you?'

'Don't listen to him, Saffy,' said Pup.

But Roly's words had gone deep. She had once been loved. She had been young, cute and puppyish. Her coat had been sleek and golden and she could run like the wind. But now she was just a smelly old dog. Who could love her now?

Pup watched the humans come, walking down between the kennels, stopping and looking at the dogs. He could barely contain his excitement. Humans so close, looking at him, bending down to talk to him through the bars. But they never stopped long beside him. He heard the words, *handsome dog, beautiful, but too big.*

Person after person passed, and Pup watched them go. It didn't seem to matter how straight he sat, or how much he wagged his tail – people looked in, smiled, but walked on by.

One young girl looked in at him. She couldn't be much younger than his boy. She was clutching something against her chest. She looked deep and hard into Pup's eyes.

The adult with her stopped and read a sign on Pup's door. 'Buster's too big, Clemmie. Not for us. See, he needs plenty of training.'

The girl walked on and gazed in Saffy's kennel. 'Hello,' she whispered to Saffy, who was curled with her back to the world. At first Saffy didn't move, but then the girl called her again. Saffy turned. She saw kind human eyes looking into hers, and she remembered a time when warm hands had stroked her fur. She remembered a time, so long ago, when she had been loved. The girl reached her fingers through the bars and Saffy hobbled over and licked them and the girl screwed up her nose and smiled.

The mother glanced at the sign on her kennel, then crouched down and looked in. 'This one's too old, Clemmie. Let's go on.'

But the girl didn't move. She stared into Saffy's eyes and Saffy stared back, and as Pup watched, he felt something pass between them. Maybe this was what Roly had meant. The look that connected them both. An invisible bond.

One of the Aprons bent down. 'We've called her Annie. She's a lovely dog. Do you want to stroke her?'

The girl nodded and she was led into the kennel where she sat beside Saffy, stroking her soft ears.

The girl's mother crouched down too. 'But she's so old.'

'So was Grandma,' said the girl. 'But we still loved her.'

The mother smiled and sat with her daughter and Saffy

167

until the bell marked the end of the visiting session and the Lookers were told it was time to go.

'So they actually want the old fleabag!' said Roly. 'Miracles can happen.'

'Why don't they take her now?' asked Pup.

'They have to be checked first, the humans that is, to make sure they have a good home to give,' said Roly.

Pup turned to look at Saffy. 'You might have a home, Saffy. You might have a human of your own.'

Saffy thumped her tail on the ground. She thought of being stolen from the home she once loved. She thought of all the pups she'd lost, and losing her beloved, damaged Reynard. 'Look, the girl's left something,' she said. She sniffed at the soft toy the girl had hugged against her chest.

'What is it?' asked Pup.

Saffy picked it up gently in her mouth and placed it protectively between her paws. 'It's a fox,' she said. 'A small red fox.'

Chapter 21
A HOWL WITH NOWHERE TO GO

'YOU SEE?' SAID SAFFY TO Rex. 'Miracles can happen. There is someone for each of us. Even me.'

Rex lifted his head to look at Saffy. 'I have no faith in humans. I have seen them at their worst. They all betray us in the end.'

'It's not true,' said Saffy. 'Please, Rex, please do what the Aprons ask. Surely it's what all of us wish for, deep down. Just to be loved simply for being ourselves.'

Rex curled his head into his flank again and closed his eyes. 'I wish for a place where there are no humans. When I close my eyes, I see myself in our safe place, running along the sand where the ocean meets the sky at the very end of the world. It is all I can think about now.'

Pup paced his kennel. 'Maybe one day when we are out of this place we can find it together,' he said. 'Please do what the Aprons ask. And when we are out of this place we can meet you there.'

'Maybe,' said Rex. He pushed his nose into his fur again and closed his eyes. 'But it won't be in this lifetime.'

And that afternoon, when the Lookers had left, the other dogs were taken to the outside runs for their exercise. Pup and Saffy stayed close together letting the cold wind ruffle their fur. When they returned inside, Rex's kennel was empty. The floor had been cleaned and the bed washed and replaced.

It was as if Rex had never existed.

Saffy spun around, trying to see if Rex had been moved to a different kennel. 'Rex?' she barked. 'Where are you? Rex? Rex?'

Pup just stared at the folded blanket. He felt an ache deep, deep in his chest. He knew he would never see his friend again.

Brave, fierce Rex had gone.

'Told you,' said Roly, eyeing them from his kennel. 'That's what happens to Forbiddens and biters. They go through the Door and have the needle. The needle that puts you to sleep and you never wake up. No one can trust a biter.'

Pup spun around. 'I trusted him,' he snarled.

'I'd put your teeth away,' said Roly. 'Or the same will happen to you.'

'Ignore him,' said Saffy softly. 'Rex gave his life for us. He knew what would happen if he got caught by the Snatchers, but still he tried to save us. He was a true friend. I will never forget him.' She picked up the toy fox that the girl had given her and curled herself around it. She closed her eyes and tried to escape into sleep.

Pup couldn't sleep. He paced in his kennel, up and down. He wanted to curl up next to Saffy. He wanted to run with Rex. He wanted to find his old friend Frenchi. But he couldn't do anything. He was stuck between wire and concrete. He felt the loss of Rex through every bone and muscle in his body. He hadn't even been able to say goodbye. Thoughts tumbled and flashed through his mind. Was it possible that humans could take Rex's life from him? How could humans do that? It wasn't theirs to take.

The feelings built up inside him and he threw back his head and howled. A cry rising up above Dogsdoom into the night air. And as he howled, others joined in too. But Pup's howl rose up above the others, calling for his friend.

It was a cry of pain from the heart, unheard and unanswered.

It was a howl with nowhere to go.

The next morning, Clemmie and her mother came for Saffy. Clemmie fixed a blue collar with silver sparkles around Saffy's neck and held her with a long blue lead.

Saffy stopped at Pup's kennel to lick him on the nose through the bars. 'Hold the faith, Pup,' she said. 'There is someone out there for you. Keep up with your training. Listen well. Someone will come. Remember that, when you feel low and when there seems no hope, remember that someone will come.'

'Take care, Saffy,' said Pup.

And Pup watched Saffy leave, Clemmie's hand on Saffy's shoulder. And Pup knew that Saffy would be in a house where she was loved and wanted. He was happy for her, but when the door closed, he felt even more alone.

'Lucky old fleabag,' said Roly. 'But it wouldn't be for me.'

'Don't you want someone of your own?' said Pup.

'Why would I when I have everyone here?'

'It's not the same,' said Pup. 'It's not the same as having a human of your own.'

'Well, keep dreaming,' said Roly. 'The old fleabag might have been old, but some like the old gentle sort. And some fall for the old brown eyes. You, however, have guard dog in you. The Aprons are careful not to give you to just anyone.'

'Why?' said Pup.

'Well, let's just say some folk want dogs like you to guard them. Some want you to fight for them.'

'Fight for them?' said Pup. For the first time ever, Pup saw Roly lose his swagger. He noticed the smallest of changes. Roly's tail tucked beneath his legs and he glanced around him.

'I've only heard tales,' whispered Roly. 'But they say men make dogs fight other dogs.'

Pup blinked. He remembered Rex telling him that he had been bred to be a fighting dog. 'Why?'

'Because Rex was right,' said Roly bitterly. 'Because no human can truly be trusted. Don't get too close. You'll only get hurt or disappointed. You're safest here. Believe me.'

Pup curled up and stared at the wall. As the yaps and barks of the other dogs silenced as the night drew in, Pup didn't know what to think at all. In his dreams he saw Rex watching him, and Saffy sitting beside him. *Someone will come*, she said. *Someone will come.*

Pup woke from the other world of sleep. He knew it was just a dream as he couldn't smell Saffy or Rex.

But Saffy's words stayed with him, and he held onto them. *Someone will come.*

Someone will come.

But for how long would he have to wait?

The Boy

The boy places the small clay dog on the window sill and stares out.

He is no longer a boy, nor is he yet a man. He is between those worlds where he cannot return to the safety of childhood or escape to his own future and freedom.

It is another grey day, one of those days where all the colour has been washed out of the world.

Clouds lie low, suffocating the city.

The boy can't see beyond the rooftops or the end of the road.

He can't see beyond tomorrow.

Days and weeks blur, but nothing changes for him.

The big man's anger fills the house. It silences and separates the boy and his mother. At school he tries to slip invisible along the corridors. He wants to be unseen and unheard. There seems to be some safety in that. He seeks refuge in the quiet places, away from the noise of the world.

The days and shadows stretch out as another summer comes and goes. Sunlight spills out across the park where children laugh and play.

But for the boy, his world remains grey.

He still sits every day on the park bench, waiting, leaving a small crust of bread, hoping his dog will return. He doesn't know what else he can do.

'I'm here, Pup,' he whispers, clutching the small clay dog in his hand. 'Where are you?'

Chapter 22
MAX

Days rolled into nights and nights rolled into days. The grey walls stared back at Pup. If it wasn't for the time spent outside during his training sessions, he wouldn't know how long he'd been in Dogsdoom. But he saw the spring turn through summer, autumn, winter and back to spring again. A few people had shown interest in him, but the Aprons were careful. They said the person for him had to be the right person.

'I said you'd be here for ever,' said Roly, when people passed him by.

But Pup still clung to Saffy's words.

Someone will come.

And as the trees burst into leaf again, her words came true.

That someone did come.

The man was young.

He hadn't stopped at any of the other kennels, like the other Lookers had done. He had walked straight up to Pup's kennel, crouched down and looked in. He had an energy about him, Pup thought. A bit like Clown, always ready to play, but a bit like Rex too, intent and serious.

'Hey, boy!' said the man.

Pup sat down with his paws together and looked back at him. He wanted to see the spark Saffy had with Clemmie. Maybe it was there, maybe it would come. Pup couldn't tell.

One of the Aprons stood behind the man. 'This is Buster.'

The man nodded. 'I read his profile on the website.'

'He needs training and an experienced owner,' said the Apron.

The man nodded again. 'My dad had German shepherds when I was younger. My dog, Floss, was an intelligent dog.'

The Apron crouched beside him. 'Buster hasn't finished his training yet so anyone who took him on would need to see us regularly.'

The man smiled. 'That's cool. Can I get him out?'

The Apron opened the door and Pup wasn't sure what to do. The man offered his hand and Pup sniffed it.

'Come on, Buster,' said the man.

And Pup stepped outside his kennel and let the man stroke his ears.

'Why don't you take him for a walk in the courtyard, to get to know him a bit,' said the Apron. She slipped a lead over Pup's neck and the man led him outside, and Pup walked at his heels all the time.

Out in the courtyard one of the other Aprons joined the man. 'So you're interested in Buster? An intelligent dog. See what he does for you.'

Pup had learned the commands, to sit, to lie down and to wait and to fetch. He did every single one with the man, his ears alert for the next command. It was fun to keep his mind working, away from the boredom of pacing in the kennel. He sat and barked for the man to throw the ball again.

'He's a smart one,' said the man.

'He seems to like you,' said the Apron.

The man smiled. 'Can I come back and see him again?'

The Apron nodded. 'If you decide to take him on, there'll be lots of home checks and follow-up checks. Dogs like these often end up in the wrong hands.'

The man ruffled Pup's fur. 'He's the one.' He walked Pup back to his kennel, shut the door and crouched down. 'You and me are going to have some adventures together. I'm Max, by the way.'

Pup watched Max go. It hadn't been the moment Roly had spoken of, of knowing a bond between him and Max. But maybe it would grow. Maybe it would take time. Maybe it wouldn't matter. At least he would be free.

Roly watched Pup from his kennel. 'You too,' he said. 'I don't believe it. First the old fleabag, then you.'

'I'm going to have a person of my own,' said Pup.

'Just don't mess up,' said Roly, turning his back on him. 'If you end up back here, you'll be heading where your friend Rex went.'

Pup stayed awake long into the night. He wouldn't mess up. He would stay loyal and true. Saffy had been right. He wouldn't be in Dogsdoom for ever.

Someone would come.

Someone *had* come.

And Pup couldn't wait to leave.

Max lived on the far side of the city, in a clean tree-lined street with tall white houses. He parked his car and opened the door.

Pup stepped out, blinking in the bright light. It had been

178

a year since he had seen the outside world. The richness of all the different smells filled his nose. The sounds of traffic and music from a house drowned the silence in his head. His feet touched the cold pavement and the wind ruffled his fur. Everything seemed too loud and too bright. He had been so used to being confined to a kennel that he wasn't sure if he was ready for the world.

He was relieved when Max led him down steps into a garden apartment. It was cool and quiet inside and smelled of Max. Pup felt safer with four walls around him.

'Well,' said Max. 'This is me.'

Pup walked around the flat. It was a long time since he had been inside a human's house. He sniffed at the sofa in the living room, and then walked through to a big bright room with large glass doors that overlooked the garden. There was a long table in the room and piles of papers. 'This is my office,' said Max. 'This is where I do most of my work.' He pointed to a dog bed on the floor. 'And this is where you can sleep.' He pointed to two other rooms. 'That's my bedroom, and that's the spare.' He closed the door to the spare room. 'You can't go in there because Mother sleeps there when she comes to visit and she says she's allergic to dog hair. She doesn't like dogs much. She said she left my dad because he loved his dogs more than he loved her.' He laughed. 'She says that I'm mad to take you on, and she'd say I'm even madder if she could hear me talk to you like this. She won't come and stay now because of you.' He scratched behind Pup's ear and whispered, 'I consider that a bonus! No more nagging!'

Pup wandered into the kitchen and sniffed around. Water was dripping from the tap and so he put his paws on the sink and licked the drops.

Max laughed again. 'You are smart. And I forgot water,' he said, filling up a bowl. He sat back and watched Pup drink. 'We'll go to the park soon, but first you need this.' Max reached into a bag and brought out a collar of soft brown leather. 'It has a disc with your name and my telephone number, so if you get lost, people know you belong to me.'

Pup let Max put the collar on him and adjust the buckle. It had been a long time since he had worn a collar. It felt safe. It meant he felt he belonged to someone, and that someone belonged to him. He wasn't a street dog any more.

Max ruffled his fur. 'This is your home now, with me. And I hope you love to run, because that's what I love to do too.'

Days slipped into weeks, and weeks slipped into months and Pup slipped into a comfortable life with Max. He felt a part of the world again. At six every morning, Pup would fetch Max's trainers and bark at him to put them on, and then they would go out across the road to the park where they would run and run.

Pup loved running as much as Max. He felt his legs grow strong and he loved the feel of the ground rushing beneath his paws. Max was a fast runner, and Pup loved to lope alongside him, his tongue hanging out as he ran along the lakeside and up into the woods behind the park. Max didn't need to put Pup on the lead any more, and Pup always came when called.

But one day, when Max and Pup were running through the park on a late autumn afternoon, Pup caught a scent that made him stop in his tracks.

'Come on, Buster,' Max called.

But Pup put his nose in the air and sniffed, trying to remember the scent that filled him with a feeling of safety and warmth.

'Come on,' called Max again, whistling for Pup to follow.

But Pup had to follow the scent. He left the path and set off across the grass, with Max trying to keep up.

The scent led him to a glade of trees, where a young child and her mother were having a picnic beneath a tree. A red-checked tablecloth was spread out on the grass and a yellow Labrador lay beside the girl, with a small toy fox held between her paws.

'Saffy!' cried Pup, bouncing up to her and licking her face.

The girl's mother tried to chase him away, but the girl just smiled. 'It's Annie's friend from the kennels.'

'You were right, Saffy,' said Pup. 'Someone did come.'

Saffy licked Pup on the nose, 'It's good to see you, Pup.'

'Buster!' Max called. He slipped the lead on Pup and apologized to the girl's mother. 'He doesn't usually run off like that.' And he turned to lead Pup away.

'Stay safe, my dear Pup,' Saffy called after him.

'You too,' Pup called back to her. 'You too.'

*

By day, Pup would curl up at Max's feet and sometimes he joined him in going through the streets to an office where Max worked with other people. And they always loved to see Pup, making him shake paws and giving him treats. By night, Pup would curl up in his dog bed, safe and warm.

Pup learned new tricks too. He discovered how to pull the handle on a door to open it. He could prise the fridge door open with his teeth and help himself to lumps of cheese and packets of ham. If he didn't want to do something, he learned that he could lie down and refuse to move so that Max had to drag him across the floor by his feet.

'You're a smart one,' Max would say, scratching Pup's head. 'Mother nags me that I should find someone to settle down with. What do you think?'

Pup put his head on one side and whined.

'Exactly what I said,' said Max. 'I'm quite happy here, just the two of us. There's no one to tell us what to do. We can eat what we like and do what we like. No need to change anything. Ever.'

'Uff!' barked Pup. He liked things as they were. He didn't want anything to change either. 'Uff! Uff!' he barked.

But neither Pup nor Max could know the change that was coming.

Chapter 23
A RUN IN THE PARK

As THE WINTER GAVE WAY to spring, and the days grew longer, Max took to running in the evenings too. Pup loved the evening runs. There were more people and dogs, more exciting sights and sounds and smells. Sometimes he caught the scent of Saffy and knew she had passed through the park. Sometimes the sight of a French bulldog would make him sniff the air, though he never caught sight or scent of Frenchi.

Max often jogged and talked on his phone or pressed at the screen as he ran. He seemed obsessed by the device in his hand, and Pup had got used to Max staring at it for hours.

But Pup didn't mind. He loved to go running. Max fed him well and he felt stronger than he had ever done before. He had grown a little higher in the shoulder, but he had filled out and didn't look so long and leggy any more. He could pull Max over in a game of tug-of-war. But he loved nothing better than to stretch out and run. When he was running he could forget all about the worries that crowded his mind when he tried to sleep. He could forget about Frenchi and Rex and Dogsdoom. Most of all, he could forget his boy. Running cleared his mind and set him free.

Max seemed to be more preoccupied lately on his phone, even when he ran. *Work stuff*, he'd grumble to Pup. *I wish I was a dog sometimes. You don't have to do any of this.*

Maybe that's why Max didn't see the woman on the

path alongside the lake. Pup ran around her, but Max was reading something on his phone and ran full speed into her. She sprawled on the ground, her bags tipped up, spilling their contents over the path.

'You complete idiot,' snapped the woman. She sat up and blood oozed through the rip in her tights. 'I thought I'd be safer walking through the park than along the roads. Seems I was wrong.'

'I'm so sorry,' said Max.

Pup licked her face and the woman pushed him away.

'My dog's OK,' said Max.

'It's not him I'm worried about,' said the woman. 'It's you.'

'Really, I'm so sorry,' said Max again. He held out his hand. 'I'll help you up.'

She glared at him, looking him up and down. She struggled to her feet and winced as she put weight on one foot. 'I'll be fine. There should be a law against people like you on your phones all the time. You should be looking where you're going.'

'Let me carry your bag and walk you home at least,' said Max.

The woman stared at him, hand on hip. 'I'm not going home. I'm going to work. Though I might not be much use as a waitress with a leg like this. I hope you haven't cost me my job.'

Max watched her hobble away. He stroked Pup on the head. 'God, I'm an idiot. Perhaps Mother's right after all. I'll have to change my ways if I want anyone to like me.'

Pup stared after the woman. Humans were crazy, he thought. They seemed only to listen to each other's words. What they said with their bodies was a different thing entirely.

Pup could tell the woman and Max actually liked each other.

They liked each other a lot.

The next evening, when Max and Pup did their loop of the park and the lake, Pup saw the woman walking alongside the lake. She had her foot in a rigid boot and walked with a stick. He left Max's side and bounded up to her.

'Oh, it's you again,' she said. But despite her cross words she bent forward and gave Pup a scratch behind the ear. 'And look, here comes your human.'

'Buster! Buster! Heel, boy,' yelled Max. He jogged up to the woman and pulled out a lead. 'I'm sorry, he's usually much more under control.'

The woman looked at him. 'It's not him that needs to be kept under control.'

Max's face flushed. 'Look I'm really sorry about yesterday . . .'

'I'm in this boot for two weeks,' said the woman.

'Did you lose your job because of me?' asked Max.

The woman softened. 'Luckily my boss likes me and they're short-staffed at the moment.'

'I was such an idiot,' said Max. 'I'm sorry.'

The woman stroked Pup's head. 'I guess you can't be that much of an idiot if your dog likes you.' She looked up and

186

smiled. 'My father has big dogs on his farm in Poland to keep the wolves away. My favourite one was called Mika. He followed me everywhere and protected me.'

'My dog's name is Buster,' said Max.

'Well, you're lucky to have Buster to look out for you,' she said. 'I'm Zofia.'

Max smiled. 'I'm Max.' He glanced across at the booth still selling snacks and drinks. 'Well, maybe Buster and I could buy you a coffee and walk you across the park to say sorry for yesterday.'

Zofia smiled. 'Sounds fair to me.'

Over the following weeks Max and Pup met up with Zofia each evening and walked with her across the park. At weekends she joined them for walks out in the green beyond the city. And as the summer moved into autumn, so Zofia moved into Max's house.

Pup loved it too. There were now two humans who looked after him and made a fuss of him. Where Max was active and always on the go, Zofia was laid-back, and fussed over Pup, stroking him and letting him lie on the sofa when Max was out. She sneaked little treats to him. And when Max and Pup went running, Zofia joined them too. Life was comfortable and easy. The autumn storms brought back memories of Frenchi and Dead Dog Alley, but Pup forced them away. It did no good to remember what he had lost. Four summers had now passed since Frenchi had found him. He hoped Frenchi had found a good home too. This was Pup's life now, with these two humans. He was safe and warm, with enough to eat. He was lucky. Very lucky. And he'd try not to let anything change it.

But another change did come. As the winter turned through into spring, Pup could feel a change in Zofia. She seemed more tired and didn't want to take Pup out for long walks. She didn't join them on runs through the park. She smelled different too and spent time in the bathroom where Pup could hear her retching over the toilet basin.

Pup lay down outside the door and whined, turning his head from side to side at the sound of Zofia being ill.

Max crouched down next to Pup. 'Hey, Buster, what's up?'

Pup scratched at the bathroom door and whined.

'You're worried about Zofia?'

Pup whined again.

Max laughed. 'She's not ill,' he said, ruffling Pup's fur. 'She's expecting our baby. You'll have someone else to look after soon too.'

Chapter 24
BABY LENA

Baby Lena arrived in an October storm that rattled the windows and brought down trees. When Max and Zofia brought her home from the hospital wrapped in a blanket and asleep in a car-seat, Pup could smell the newness and the smallness of the squirming infant in front of him. Her snuffles and cries brought back long-lost puppy memories of needing to feel safe and warm. Something deep inside of him knew he had to protect her. She was family, part of the pack. He felt the same bond he had had with his boy, the same love. He hadn't been able to protect his boy, but Pup was bigger now, and he would look after this small human. He would guard her with his life.

Pup followed Zofia wherever she went with Lena. If she sat on the sofa to feed her, Pup slept at her feet. At night Pup would lie next to the cot, and if Max or Zofia took Lena away without him, he would fret until they returned. If people came to the door, he barked louder than before, and when the health visitor came to check on Lena, she insisted Zofia must lock him away.

'Buster loves Lena,' said Zofia. 'He won't leave her alone.'

'He's a big dog,' said the health visitor. 'And dogs can be unpredictable.'

'He wouldn't do anything to harm her,' said Zofia.

'You never know,' said the health visitor. 'You can never trust a dog.'

That night Max's mother said the same thing on the phone.

'You just don't know,' Max's mother repeated. 'You can never trust a dog. You should send him back to the dogs' home. You might regret it if you don't.'

'Mum, Buster is fine. He's part of the family,' said Max. 'Zofia and I wouldn't have met if it hadn't been for him.'

Max could sense his mother bristling down the phone. She didn't approve of dogs. She hadn't approved of Zofia either. She'd had other aspirations for her son. *Why don't you find a nice English girl?* she had said when Max had first mentioned Zofia. But she had a granddaughter now and somehow that made up for her disappointment.

'I've decided to come and stay at the end of the week,' said Max's mother. 'I can be on hand to help you both out.'

'Great,' lied Max. 'But we're a bit of a squash. We've only two bedrooms and Lena has one of them.'

'I'll sleep on the sofa,' said Max's mum. 'And I'll stay as long as you want.'

'But you don't like Buster,' said Max.

'You can keep him out of the way,' she said. 'You can lock him in the utility room.'

Max put the phone down and looked at Zofia. 'I couldn't stop her.'

'Please tell me she's only coming for one day,' said Zofia.

'She's coming to stay,' said Max.

'What about Buster?' said Zofia. 'She says she's allergic to dogs.'

Max shrugged his shoulders. 'Maybe she'll decide not to stay for very long after all.'

*

When Max's mother bundled into the house with bags, Pup felt unease settle across the house. He could sense Zofia was wary of Max's mother.

'Call me Janice,' Max's mother had insisted. She smiled but her body said otherwise.

Instead of being relaxed, Zofia was tense. Lena seemed to pick up on the changed atmosphere in the house too and cried more often.

Pup fretted, pacing about the house, not quite sure where to sleep.

'He's making me sneeze,' Janice would say. 'You must keep him in the utility room while I'm here.'

'Have you taken your antihistamines, Mum?' asked Max.

'Yes,' sniffed Janice, 'but your dog is worse than other dogs. It's a different sort of fur.' She scratched her ankles. 'Has he got fleas?'

'No, Mum.'

'He's got wolf in him,' said Janice. 'Look at him. There's a mean look in his eyes.'

Max ruffled Pup's fur. 'Mum, Buster's fine. He loves everyone.'

But Pup didn't like Janice and kept a wide berth around her. He lay in the corner of the room watching Lena.

'It's not natural,' said Janice. 'I don't like the way he looks at the baby. Look, Lena doesn't like him. She cries a lot. Maybe that's why.'

Zofia picked up Lena in her arms and rocked her.

'You spoil that baby,' said Janice. She tutted. 'She needs to know who's in charge. She'll run rings around you if you

192

pick her up every time she cries. If you just let her cry she'll go back to sleep.'

'She's just a baby,' said Zofia. 'She needs cuddles.'

Janice raised her eyebrows. 'I've raised three children, dear. I do have some experience in the matter.'

Zofia turned away from her, but Pup could sense she wanted to get away.

'I'll take Lena out for a stroll,' said Janice. 'You need some rest.'

'No really, I'll go. I need to get out,' said Zofia. She gave Max a look. 'Buster needs to get out too.'

Max followed Zofia. 'Mum means well. She's trying to help.'

'Well, she's not,' said Zofia. 'Buster doesn't like her. She keeps shutting him away.'

'She's allergic to dogs,' said Max.

'Well, maybe I'm allergic to your mother,' snapped Zofia.

Max scowled at her. 'That's unfair, Zofia. Lena's her only grandchild. You could try to get along with my mother. Why don't you go with her to the park?'

'I want to go with Buster. He's better company.'

'Zofia!'

Zofia lay Lena in the buggy and pushed her way out of the door.

Pup trotted alongside Zofia as she stormed through the park. The bumping motion of the baby buggy over the rough ground sent Lena to sleep and Zofia slowed down as her thoughts settled. She sat down on a bench at the far end of the park and drew Pup into her arms. She buried her head into Pup's fur and cried hot tears. 'Oh, Buster, thank goodness I've got you. You understand, don't you?'

Pup licked the tears on her face.

Rain started to fall and Zofia pulled the plastic rain-cover over Lena and drew the hood up on her coat. She ran her hands along Pup's ears. 'Lena's lucky to have you too,' she said. 'When Lena's older, I'm going to tell her a different version of *Little Red Riding Hood*.' She started giggling. 'I'm going to tell her how the big brave wolf ate Grandma, how he gobbled her all up and everyone lived happily ever after.'

'Uff!' woofed Pup, because he could tell Zofia was happy again. 'Uff!'

And Zofia turned her head up to the rain and burst into wild laughter. She laughed and laughed, and she didn't stop until an elderly man came to check if she was OK.

The rain fell harder and a cold wind blew, so Zofia made her way back home with Pup trotting close by the buggy's side all the way. 'Lena will be lucky to have the best friend ever,' said Zofia. 'I can imagine all the things you'll get up to together.' She took a deep breath before slipping the key in the door. She turned to Pup. 'It's only a few days with Janice. If you can put up with her, then so can I.'

Pup watched his people carefully. Janice took over the house, barking orders, thinking she was top dog. Zofia said nothing but was wary of Janice. She avoided her when she could. Max ran between Janice and Zofia, not wanting to upset one or the other but somehow irritating them both.

And little Lena was in the middle of this all, baby Lena, who Pup loved with all his heart and soul.

'Mum has offered to babysit Lena so we can go out for the afternoon together,' said Max.

'It's my last day here,' said Janice, 'so you may as well make use of me.'

'I'm fine,' said Zofia. 'I don't need to go out.'

'Rubbish,' said Janice. 'It'll be good for you and Max to have some time together.'

'She's right,' said Max. 'Just the two of us. We could go to the cinema.'

'What about Buster?' said Zofia.

'He'll be fine in the utility room until we get back,' said Max. He ruffled Pup's fur. 'We won't be long.'

Janice eyed Pup warily.

'Come on, Zofia,' urged Max. 'It'll do us good.'

Zofia relented, but she made sure she had everything in place for Lena.

Max shut Pup in the utility room with a bowl of water and some food. 'Won't be long, Buster. Be good.'

Pup heard Zofia's and Max's voices fade. He put his paws on the window sill and looked out to see them walking down the road together, and he felt a tight knot inside. They hadn't been gone for long when Pup heard Lena begin to cry. He heard Janice pacing up and down talking to Lena, but Lena's cries became louder and louder and more strident. Pup felt his heart thumping in his chest. Lena sounded scared, frightened and alone. He had to be there for her. He scratched at the door, his claws raking the wood and he barked, calling to Lena. Her cries became even louder and all Pup wanted to be was to be near her. He knew about doors, he had opened them before. He stood on his hind legs and pulled and turned the handle with his teeth until it swung wide open.

Pup rushed through the kitchen to the hallway where Janice was strapping a screaming Lena into the buggy. Janice was taking Lena out and away. Maybe away for ever, thought Pup. But Lena was safe here in this place, this den. This is where Zofia and Max would come back to. He had to stop Janice taking Lena away.

Pup's hackles rose and he placed himself between Janice and the buggy.

'Get away,' shouted Janice. She picked up an umbrella from the stand and waved it at him.

Pup stood his ground between Janice and Lena. A low rumbling growl came from deep inside his chest.

'Get away,' screamed Janice. She brought the umbrella down on Pup's head, but he dodged and pulled it from her.

Pup bared his teeth, but Janice would not back away. She came closer and closer and reached in for Lena. Lena's screams rose higher and higher and panic gripped Pup. Janice might be taking Lena away for ever and he had to stop her. He loved Lena. He loved her more than life itself.

Pup lunged at Janice and grabbed her arm. He wouldn't let her move. The more Janice struggled, the harder Pup held, his teeth tearing through the fabric of her sleeve until he was biting down on bare skin. But still he would not let go. He would protect Lena at all costs.

He held onto Janice and waited and waited and waited until his heart lifted when he heard Zofia's and Max's voices, and the sound of their key sliding into the door.

Chapter 25
DEAD DOG RUNNING

'HE'S A VICIOUS BRUTE,' SPAT Janice as the paramedics bandaged her hands. 'I told you, you should have got rid of him before.'

'I'm so sorry, Mum,' said Max.

'Buster didn't understand,' said Zofia. 'He was trying to protect Lena.'

Janice glared at her. 'That dog is unpredictable. It could have been Lena. You have to get rid of him.'

'No!' said Zofia.

'Well, I ask you,' fumed Janice. 'What kind of mother are you, if you put a dog before your child?'

Max put a hand on Zofia's arm. 'I rang the dog kennels. They agree. It's too much of a risk. They can take him back.'

'Max!' said Zofia. 'How can we?'

'I know,' said Max, gripping Zofia's hand. 'I hate it too. But just imagine, Zofia! Just imagine if it had been Lena. What then? We'd never forgive ourselves.'

'Sense at last,' said Janice, triumphant. 'Besides, you don't want a dog while you are bringing up a child. All that dirt and dog hair too. You'll see. Soon you'll forget all about him. It'll be best in the end.'

The Aprons from Dogsdoom arrived in the early evening to collect Pup. Their scent came through the utility room windows as they walked to the door. Pup's heart filled with fear and the howling emptiness of Dogsdoom. What would happen to him now? He was a biter. He couldn't be trusted.

200

Zofia bent down and wrapped her arms around Pup's neck and sobbed. She smelled of the warm scent of Lena. 'I'm sorry, Buster.' She wept into his fur. 'I'm so sorry.'

Pup licked her face.

'I'll never forget you. I'll tell Lena all about you,' Zofia said. 'I'll tell her the truth. And I'll tell her the story about the big brave wolf who ate Grandma, because he wanted to protect the child he loved.'

Max slipped through into the room with one of the Aprons from Dogsdoom. His eyes were red from crying. 'It's time,' he said.

'A shame,' said the Apron. 'I remember him when he was with us in the kennels. A lovely dog. But you can't be too careful. Especially when there's kids around.' The Apron pulled out a muzzle and began to slide it over Pup's nose.

'It's OK,' said Max. 'He won't need it. I'll lead him out.' He bent down and undid Pup's collar, laying it on the floor, and he put the slip-lead around Pup's neck. 'I'm sorry, boy.'

Pup sniffed at the collar on the floor, feeling lost and un-owned again.

Un-wanted.

'I can't watch him go,' said Zofia.

Pup felt his muscles tighten and his heart thump inside his chest. Worry ran through him.

Janice was in the living room, holding Lena against her chest as Max led him out. Pup didn't even get a chance to push his nose against Lena's soft warm skin and say goodbye. He sat down refusing to move, but Max pulled the lead hard. 'Come on, Buster.'

The Aprons walked ahead to the waiting van. Pup's mind filled with the memories of when he, Rex and Saffy had been bundled into the van. He thought of the dark kennels and the noise. The thoughts suffocated him. He would never be able to see the stars. The tug on the slip-lead pulled tight against his throat. He couldn't go back. He couldn't.

'Come on,' urged Max, pulling him towards the waiting van.

The van meant Dogsdoom, caged and trapped. He was a biter now and Dogsdoom meant only one thing.

The Door.

Anger rose in Pup's chest. Rex had been right. Humans always let you down in the end. Always.

'Come on, Buster,' said Max. 'Good boy.'

Pup followed Max towards the van.

But he wouldn't let them take him back to Dogsdoom.

He was a dead dog to them now.

Rex was right. He owed humans nothing.

Nothing at all.

When Max tried to heave him into the van, Pup spun around and bit down hard on Max's hand, his teeth sinking into Max's skin, forcing him to let go of the lead.

Then Pup turned and ran.

He ran and ran.

A dead dog running.

Running for his life.

Chapter 26
REMEMBERED SUNSHINE

PUP RAN BLINDLY.

Cars screeched to a halt and blasted their horns at him as he sprinted across roads. He leaped over gardens behind houses and on through the leafy roads and towards the rumbling heart of the city where he found some comfort in the dark alleyways and back streets.

He stopped only when he could run no more, when his feet were sore and his heart pounded in his ears and when he could no longer draw breath. He slumped down in an alleyway that sheltered him from the raw November rain. The slip-lead had pulled tighter around his neck and he clawed at it with his feet, pulling it loose and over his head. His mouth was dry, and hunger gnawed at his belly. At the end of the alleyway he could hear cars pass and sirens and the noises of the city. He was a street dog again. But he felt lost without a pack. He looked up to the sky to seek the dog star for company, but the night was covered in cloud.

He was utterly alone.

He wondered if Frenchi, Clown and Merle were still in the city. Maybe they were back under the railway arches waiting for him. Pup set off again, hidden by the darkening sky. People hurried along pavements, keen to get out of the rain. They didn't notice the big dog slip by in the shadows. He trotted through the park where Frenchi had taken him on his first day as a street dog. All the scents came back to him, reminding him of his days at the Railway Den. He began to trot even faster, thinking about the times with Merle and Clown at markets, and the evenings sitting in sunshine with Saffy and Reynard, and the wild winter nights when Rex and Lady Fifi protected them all inside the den. He wanted to curl up next to Frenchi and fall asleep with his head on Frenchi's chest, listening to his rumbling snores.

He slowed as he neared the road alongside the railway arches. He couldn't catch any scent of Frenchi, Merle or Clown. Maybe the Sewer Dogs had moved into the Railway Den. As Pup crept closer in the shadows, he could see the Railway Den had changed. The bush beside the loose panel had been pulled away, and the wooden boards had been replaced by steel shutters. There was no sign or scent of the others.

There was no one there for him.

He remembered Frenchi once saying: *a dog on his own, is no dog at all.*

Pup felt emptiness rip through him like the cold autumn wind. He couldn't stay. He wanted to be as far away as possible. He ran, and kept running. He let his mind become numb. He wasn't even aware of where he was going. Houses, shops, garages passed by in a blur. This was a part of the city he had never been through before. A car slammed to a stop as he crossed a road, the bumper catching his back legs and sending him tumbling against wire railings. Someone climbed out of the car, but Pup didn't want to be caught, so he slipped through a gap between loose railings and limped away.

He found himself in the darkness of a park, his feet

touching soft grass. Pain jolted through his leg, but he could put some weight on it, and he hobbled away from the street lights, wanting to find somewhere to hide and curl up and sleep. The rain was coming down harder now and Pup felt as if all his energy had been drained out of him. He walked deeper and deeper into the park, following a path that wound between the trees, and as he walked, his feet seemed to know the twists and turns. Did he know this park? Had he come here with Max? It sparked a memory of remembered sunshine, of running in shafts of sunlight. In his mind he saw his boy ahead of him, calling him on. He couldn't tell if he was awake or asleep, but he kept walking, putting one foot in front of the other.

He stopped at a park bench and caught the scent of remembered sunshine, of football socks and cheese puffs. It was an old scent, maybe a few days old. He snuffled around the base of the bench and found a small scrap of bread, soggy from the rain. He looked up and kept walking. The path seemed to draw him, and with it the remembered route through the park and out to the other side, following a memory that took him through an industrial estate, past a row of shops and down a road with terraced houses.

Pup broke into a limping trot. He knew this place. He passed the small front gardens, some paved, some overgrown with weeds. He remembered feeling small again, being a small pup trying to keep up with his boy. His feet stopped at one door and he sniffed. He knew this door.

The remembered scents filled his nose.

Was it too much to hope his boy was here?

'Uff!' he barked. He scratched on the door. 'Uff! Uff! Uff!' *Let me in. Let me in. Let me in.*

No one answered. The night was dark, and the wind whirled along the road. There were no lights on in the houses and curtains were drawn shut. Somewhere a siren blared into the night.

'UFF, UFF, UFF,' barked Pup.

A door further down the road opened and a man looked out, the light from his doorway slicing into the darkness.

Pup scratched on the door in front of him again, threw back his head and howled.

The door swung open and a figure stood silhouetted by the light.

Pup fell silent. The figure smelled of his boy, but this boy was much taller than Pup remembered. He backed away.

The person bent down. 'Pup? Is that you?'

This boy's voice was deeper too. He stretched out his hand and Pup sniffed it.

Pup crept closer. This was his boy, unmistakably his boy. But the boy he knew wasn't tall like this. But many summers had passed and Pup was no longer a small pup. Maybe his boy was no longer a small boy.

'Pup? Is that you?' said the boy again.

Pup pushed his nose into his boy's hands.

It was his boy.

His boy.

Here.

Now.

Pup's chest felt as if it might burst. His tail wagged so

hard his whole body swung from side to side. He couldn't stop. 'My boy, my boy, my boy,' he whined and yelped, trying to jump into his boy's arms.

'Oi!' The voice came from the neighbour. 'Is that your dog?'

'Sorry,' said the boy, pulling Pup inside.

The man said something else, but his boy shut the door.

His boy wrapped his arms around Pup and buried his head into his neck and sobbed, hot tears sliding into Pup's fur.

A woman came down the stairs and stood in the hallway, rubbing the sleep from her eyes. 'Kieran, what's going on? It's the middle of the night!'

The boy looked at his mother, but he didn't let go of Pup.

'It's Pup,' he said. 'He's come back.'

The mother eyed Pup warily. 'Pup?'

His boy was still crying. 'My dog. The dog you took from me when I was ten.'

'It can't be,' said his mother.

'It is,' said his boy. 'I'd know him anywhere.'

'He'll have to go,' she said.

'He's my dog,' shouted the boy. 'He belongs to me.'

Heavy footsteps sounded on the stairs and Pup looked up to see the big man staring at him.

The boy clung onto Pup, holding him against his chest. 'Pup's my dog. You're not taking him again.'

The big man said nothing at first, then took a step towards Pup. Pup was no longer a small puppy. He knew the ways of men. He could feel his boy's fear of the big man. He growled softly.

'How d'you know it's him?' said the big man.

'I just know,' said the boy. 'He knows me too.'

'He's a big dog now,' said the big man.

'He's my dog,' said the boy. 'He was always my dog.'

The big man stood his ground and didn't take his eyes from Pup. 'He can stay.'

The mother glanced between the big man and the boy. 'We can't keep dogs here, Rory.'

'He can stay,' repeated the big man.

'Really?' said the boy.

Pup watched the big man. He watched for the truth between the words. He watched the body language of the big man and it was full of threat and menace. There was something else too, something hidden in silence, and Pup didn't trust this man at all.

'He's dripping wet,' said the boy's mother.

'I'll get a towel,' said the boy, and together Pup and his boy edged past the big man and went up the stairs.

Pup led the way into the boy's room and sniffed at the jumble of clothes on the floor, then climbed onto his boy's bed.

'You remember, don't you?' said the boy. He rubbed the rain from his fur, and Pup whined when he touched his sore leg. 'What happened to you?'

The boy's mother stood in the doorway. 'He can't sleep in here. You'll have to shut him in the kitchen.'

'He'll howl like before,' said his boy. 'Besides, he's hurt.'

The boy's mother raked her hands through her hair. 'Just tonight then.'

His boy shut the door and then curled up around Pup, holding his paw in his warm human hand. He pulled a cover around them both. 'You came back, Pup. You came back. To me. And I won't let anyone ever take you away from me again.'

Pup felt exhaustion wash over him. He felt warm and safe. He felt loved. He had waited for this moment for so long, to be held within the arms of his boy.

He licked his boy's hand, too tired to lift his head. Then he let sleep engulf him.

He was home, at last.

He had found his boy.

Chapter 27
BROKEN

PUP WOKE TO THE SOUND of someone banging on the door.

'Kieran,' called his boy's mother. 'It's time for school.'

'I'm not going,' shouted his boy.

'You've got no choice,' said his mother.

Pup's boy sat up in bed and wrapped his arms around Pup. 'I'm not leaving my dog.'

The boy's mother opened the door and looked in. 'You've got to go to school.'

'Can we really keep Pup?' asked the boy.

'Rory said you can,' said his mother.

'Is he still here?'

She shook her head. 'He's gone to work. He'll be back tonight.'

The boy held onto Pup. 'Don't let Pup go anywhere. Promise me.'

'Go to school, Kieran.'

'Promise me,' insisted his boy.

'I promise,' said his mother.

The boy watched his mother in silence, and then nodded. He shut the door and changed into his school clothes. He placed the small clay dog on the bedside table.

Pup sniffed it, nudging it with his nose.

'Careful,' smiled his boy. 'I made this to remind me of you. I wished and wished on it every single day. And it brought you home.'

Pup looked at the small clay dog and knew his boy had

212

never given up hope. He knew his boy had been thinking of him too.

His boy packed a small bag with other clothes and a pair of trainers. He pushed the bag under the bed and hugged Pup. 'If Rory changes his mind when he gets back tonight, we'll run away together, you and me. I'm not letting you go again.'

Pup yawned and stretched. His leg felt better and he followed his boy into the kitchen where he shared his boy's toast. He was glad the big man wasn't in the house, but the boy's mother watched him warily.

His boy pulled on a coat and grabbed his school bag. 'I'll be back soon, Pup.'

Pup tried to follow his boy to the door, but the boy's mother insisted that Pup was shut in the bathroom. Pup felt a deep knot inside him at being left alone. He whined and barked for his boy to come back. He licked at water from the dripping tap and barked again, and when no one came he pulled the door open with his paws and wandered down the stairs. He was still hungry and thirsty. The boy's mother shut herself in the kitchen, and so Pup waited by the front door. He waited and waited to hear the key in the lock.

But when the front door opened again, it wasn't his boy.

It was the big man.

Pup shrank back from him.

'Rory, is that you?' called the boy's mother.

'Is Kieran here?' asked the big man.

The boy's mother came out of the kitchen. 'He's at school.'

'Good,' said the big man. He stared at Pup. 'I know someone who would pay a lot of money for a dog like him.' He scrolled down some addresses on his phone. 'I'll give him a ring.'

'What'll we tell Kieran?' said the boy's mother.

'Tell him what you like,' said the big man.

The boy's mother leaned back against the table. 'We'll say you got hold of his old owners. We'll say they wanted him back.'

'Like I said,' said Rory. 'Tell him what you like.'

Pup slid past them into his boy's room. He climbed onto the bed and pushed his nose into the bed covers. He didn't want to be with these two humans. He wanted his boy.

It was a while before the front door opened again, but when it did, Pup heard the voice of another man talking to the big man. Pup pricked his ears forward, but something about the conversation made his hackles rise. The two men walked into his boy's bedroom. The other man was even bigger than the big man. He had wide shoulders and a thick neck. He walked with the same slow swagger as Fang, and looked Pup directly in the eye.

Rory pointed at Pup. 'That's him.'

'Nice dog,' said the other man.

Pup curled his lip and growled, showing a line of sharp teeth.

'Told you he'll make a good guard dog,' said Rory.

'Will he fight?' said the other man.

'Look at the scars on him,' said Rory. 'He's fought before.'

'I'll give you three hundred for him,' said the other man.

'I told you five hundred,' said Rory.

'Four hundred . . .'

'Done.'

The other man counted out notes and passed a fat envelope to Rory.

Rory looked inside. 'He's yours.'

Pup growled and snarled at the two men, but they cornered him, and while Pup launched himself at the big man, the other man slipped a chain around his neck, pulling it tight, and a muzzle closed over his nose. Pup struggled and clawed at the muzzle, but the other man pushed him down, tying rope around his feet.

In the struggle, the small clay dog was knocked from the table. Pup watched as the big man's foot came down upon it and crushed it into pieces. The clay dog that his boy had made with his own hands, and wished and wished upon to bring Pup home, was broken. And in that moment, Pup felt as if his chance of being together with his boy had been destroyed. Gone, in a brief burst of violence.

Rory stood over Pup and gave him a kick in the ribs. 'Vicious mutt.'

Then Pup felt himself lifted up and carried out of the house and bundled into the boot of a waiting car. The boot slammed shut, locking Pup in darkness, and the car lurched forwards, taking him away.

It was taking Pup far, far away from his boy.

The Boy

The boy runs.

He doesn't stop running. His mother is calling his name, but he wants to be away from her and away from the big man. He runs blindly past houses and shops. Cars hoot at him as he crosses roads without looking. His heart is hammering in his chest and his lungs burn, but he can't stop running. The houses give way to fields and to smaller roads. He slows but his feet keep walking, following a road that climbs higher and higher toward the hills that rise above the city.

The evening is drawing in, and cold wind is blowing. Somewhere, far away, a siren blares out into the night. Car headlights pick him out on the road and the boy doesn't want to be seen, so he climbs over a gate following a footpath that leads up to the ridge above. It's quiet here away from the city, just the call of crows and the wind rushing through the grasses, making the trees heave and sigh.

He keeps walking until he reaches the top of the ridge. He opens his palm to look one last time at the broken pieces of clay dog, then throws them as far as he can. The wind picks them up and carries them away. A sleety rain stings the back of his neck, and so he sits with his back against a stone wall and wraps his arms around his knees.

He stares down at the city spread out before him. When he was down there, he couldn't see beyond four walls of his bedroom. But from up here, the city looks like a galaxy of stars in the gathering darkness. Beyond the city he sees more hills, and beyond those are the shining stars of other towns and villages. In the very distance lies a strip of ocean, catching the last rays of sunlight, and beyond the horizon is the rest of the universe.

He takes a deep breath and feels the small fluttering of hope inside his chest.

For the first time ever, he can see past tomorrow. This world is big and wide and waiting for him.

And he knows that he needed Pup to show him this.

Because Pup came back.

Not for anyone else.

Just for him.

Because he loved him.

The boy understands that he is important enough to be loved.

He climbs up onto the wall and stares down into the city. Pup is there somewhere, among those streets and houses. He is there. The boy cups his hands to his mouth and howls for his dog. He howls to say, 'I will never stop looking. I will find you. I love you too.'

And far, far away, an answering cry rises up into the night.

Chapter 28
IN FOR
THE KILL

PUP HURT.

His ribs hurt where the big man had kicked him. His jaw hurt where the men had tightened the muzzle, and his feet hurt from being tied together. He'd lain in the boot of the car while it had sped away over bumps and swerved around corners. He'd struggled to breathe where the boot of the car was hot and airless. It smelled of things he'd not scented before. He felt the car slow to a stop and heard the sound of metal gates being opened and shut, and chains being dragged across.

Pup was hauled out of the boot into bright sunlight. He wanted his boy. How would his boy find him now? The man pulled the ropes off Pup's feet and put a chain around his neck again. When he yanked the chain, the blunt metal spikes dug into Pup's skin. The man pulled the muzzle from Pup's nose and Pup rubbed it with his paws, trying to ease the soreness. When the man stepped towards him, Pup curled his lip, but before he knew it, the chain tightened, digging the spikes into his neck again.

The man booted Pup in the ribs. 'Don't mess with me, dog.'

Pup backed away.

Another man came over. 'What's that, Shane, a wolf?'

Shane laughed. 'More like a werewolf. Ugly brute. That's what I'll call him. The Werewolf.'

The other man laughed too. 'I reckon The Werewolf will make you some serious money.'

The place Pup found himself in was a closed yard with high walls and metal gates. Pup couldn't tell where it was but thought it must be somewhere in the city. He could hear the trains rumbling in the distance and the hum of a road busy with traffic. Shane chained Pup to a metal post and stood back and looked at him. 'We'll soon see what you're made of.'

That night Pup listened to the wind that rattled the gates and blew litter up into the air. He thought he heard a distant cry calling to him from far, far away. He threw his head to the sky and howled back too.

Pup was chained up all day and all night. One night became two, and two became three and soon Pup wasn't sure how many nights he had been in the yard. He was often left for hours alone. There was no one in the yard at night. It was just him. When the rain came, Pup had no shelter and so he curled up with his back to the wind and his nose in his tail. He lapped at water in puddles as Shane often forgot to put down water for him to drink. As the winter months wore on, Pup's fur grew thick to keep out the cold. All he could do was to pace the circle around the metal post. Shane didn't even take him for walks to relieve himself. He just hosed down the concrete around Pup, or never bothered at all, leaving Pup feeling dirty and unclean.

On clear nights Pup often stared up at the stars. 'Where are you, Sirius?' he would howl, his breath curling into the cold air. 'Where are you when I need you?' But the dog star shone down with a cold hard light, leaving Pup utterly alone.

The yard was busy by day. Vans and cars came and went all the time, with different people bringing things and taking other things away. Sometimes Shane would walk around with Pup and parade him up and down in front of people that came. Sometimes a visitor would stop to look at him. Pup was something to be feared, to be stared at. No humans stroked him or gave him a kind word. The humans that came to the yard were watchful and wary of each other, mixed with bravado and posturing. Sometimes they brought other dogs that were fearful and angry like their owners. But Pup kept silent. And somehow his silence protected him. His silence seemed to contain a power. He stood tall and stared out the other dogs. He could outstare humans too. Other dogs turned their eyes away from him and humans walked warily around him too. Yet he was chained and trapped, unable to escape.

Then, one cold January night, Shane came to the yard and unclipped him from the chain and put him into a van. Pup stretched his limbs, but his muscles felt weakened from being chained up for so long. The ride in the van seemed to last a long time, and after a while, Pup could smell the cool air of the green land beyond the city. There were other smells too, of strange animals, and a very bumpy track that made Pup cling with his claws to the floor of the van.

The van doors opened, and Shane pulled Pup roughly out. The moon was bright, a large ball of light rising above the trees. An owl hooted into the night and somewhere beyond a line of trees came the baying of dogs.

Pup could sense Shane was tense and nervous. He

tightened the collar around Pup and held Pup on a short lead. Someone came out of the shadows to talk to him and lead him past the line of trees to a large barn. Slivers of light cut through the barn doors across the ground.

'In here,' said the man.

Shane swaggered into the barn, holding Pup, but Pup could feel his fear. Shane was scared of who or what might be inside.

Bright lights lit up the centre of the barn where railings had been set in a circle on the dirt floor. Pup became aware of humans and dogs in the shadows around the edges.

'So this is The Werewolf,' said a voice. The owner of the voice stepped out from the shadows.

Pup could feel Shane's grip tighten on his collar, as if seeking some protection from Pup, but Pup owed Shane no loyalty.

The man ran his hand over Pup's back and laughed. 'I heard you had a wolf. This one's skin and bone. There's no power in him.'

'We'll see,' said Shane,

'How much d'you bet?' said the man.

'Five hundred quid,' said Shane.

The man laughed. 'Done.'

Pup felt tense. He sensed something wasn't right, but he didn't know what the men were planning. Shane led him into the ring and held him, while the other man brought over another dog. It was a small skinny terrier. He was black and tan in colour and had a face full of scars. The terrier, seeing Pup, pulled at his lead and went into a wild frenzy, snapping and snarling.

Pup just stared at the dog.

Both men led the dogs into the ring, unleashed them and stepped out. Other men came to crowd around the ring and look in.

The other dog was snarling at Pup, but he didn't move forward. 'Go on then,' he said, 'get it over with.'

Pup stared at the terrier, his hackles raised. 'Get what over with?'

'Attack me,' said the other dog.

Pup backed away from the dog and he heard men roar with laughter. 'Attack you, why?'

The other dog stopped growling for a moment. 'Because that's what you're meant to do. You're a fight dog.'

'A fight dog?' said Pup.

The other dog walked a circle around him. 'Don't you know?'

Pup watched him warily.

'You don't know, do you?' said the other dog. 'I'm the set-up. The man who brought me in is the Master. He sends me in. You fight me and win, and your man gets the money. He thinks he's got a winner, so he puts more money on the next fight and the Master sends his best dog in and wins the lot.'

'Money?' said Pup. 'What's that?'

'The stuff humans love,' said the dog. 'Paper that smells of a thousand hands. They do anything for it. They fight for it. They lie for it. They even die for it.'

'I don't want to fight anyone,' said Pup.

Men were shouting at both dogs.

'You don't have a choice,' said the dog. He sank his teeth into Pup's leg. The bite wasn't hard, but Pup whipped around and snarled at the dog. The dog scuttled back, his tail between his legs.

'Told you he can fight,' shouted Shane. 'Go on, Wolf.'

'Look,' said the dog, 'just make a lot of noise, come and growl and snarl at me and I'll back off and you've won, OK?' He lunged at Pup again, biting hard on Pup's tail, drawing blood.

This time, Pup bared his teeth and growled, springing forward and pinning the dog down in one swift movement. The other dog howled and whimpered, and when Pup lifted his paw, he crawled away.

'See,' shouted Shane triumphantly. 'Mine is the best dog.'

The Master handed over the money. 'Seems you was right. I'll guess you want to call it a night. Your dog looks tired.'

'He's not tired,' said Shane. 'He could fight all night.'

The Master leaned against the railings. 'Want to do another bet?' He pointed at a large dog curled up in the corner. 'I'll put in Thor.' The dog was a large cross-breed, battle-scarred with shredded ears. He had a greying muzzle and a clouded damaged eye.

'That old brute?' said Shane. 'Another five hundred quid.'

The Master shrugged his shoulders. 'I'll raise you to a thousand pounds.'

Shane seemed reluctant.

'So, you don't think your dog is that good after all?' said the Master.

The men around him laughed.

'He's the best,' said Shane, rising to the challenge. 'A thousand it is.'

Shane dragged Pup back into the ring and Pup watched as Thor was led inside. Thor was a mass of silent power. He didn't take his eyes from Pup. But Pup could tell Thor wasn't scared of him. He wasn't scared of anybody. He just looked like a dog that had a job to do and was going to get it done.

The man slipped the muzzle off and both men stepped out of the ring.

Thor stared at Pup, and Pup stared back. Thor was shorter than Pup but he was just full of muscle, thick-necked and a solid body. A low growl set up in the dog's chest.

'I won't fight you,' said Pup. 'I have no reason to fight you.'

'You do,' growled the dog.

'What reason?' said Pup.

'Because I'm going to kill you,' said Thor. 'But you will die whether you fight me or not.'

Pup began to slowly circle around the dog. 'We don't have to fight each other,' he said.

Thor peeled back his lips, showing a mouthful of sharp teeth, and he charged at Pup. The speed of him took Pup by surprise and the weight of Thor knocked him off his feet. Pup sprawled across the ground. He tried to get up but Thor was on him, him teeth grabbing Pup by the ear. Pup yelped and pulled away, feeling his ear rip. He struggled sideways, but Thor's teeth bit deep into his leg and he shook and dragged him backwards. It was all happening so fast.

Anywhere Pup tried to escape, Thor was there, snarling and growling and biting Pup again and again. Pup tried to stand, but pain shot through him. He tried to scrabble beneath the railings, but Shane's boot kicked him back into the ring.

'Get back in there, you filthy coward,' screamed Shane. 'Fight!'

There was no escape.

Pup was no match for this dog.

Pup was bitten and mauled until he was left lying exhausted in the dirt.

He tried to stand, but Thor pinned him down.

Then Thor opened his jaws wide, and went in for the kill.

Chapter 29
SERVANTS OF MEN

'ENOUGH, THOR!'

Pup watched as Thor's owner threw a rope around Thor's neck and yanked him back.

'Reckon you owe me a thousand pounds,' said the Master to Shane.

'Fight's not over yet,' said Shane.

'You want me to let Thor finish your dog off?' said the Master.

Shane spat on the ground. 'Might as well.'

'I'll do a deal,' said Thor's owner. 'It's in your favour. If you let me have your mutt, I'll only take five hundred from you. That way you've lost no money tonight.'

Shane stared at the man. 'So you recognize he's a fighter?'

'Not yet,' said the Master. 'Look at him. He's skin and bone and no muscle to him. He's needs proper training. So here's my deal. Thor can finish him off. Or you can take my offer.'

Shane nodded and handed back the money he'd won on the previous fight, then another man walked Shane out of the barn alone into the cold night.

Thor stared at Pup. 'The Master likes you. Maybe there is a fighter inside after all.'

Another man grabbed Pup and lifted him up. Pain seared through him and the world blurred at the edges. He drifted in and out of consciousness, aware he was travelling again, his body sliding and jolting in a different van. The Master lifted him out and placed him on the cold, hard ground and washed him down with a hose. The cold water washed away the blood and cleaned the wounds, but left Pup shivering beneath a winter moon.

The Master bent down. 'Let's see what you're made of when those wounds heal.' He clipped a chain around Pup's neck and walked away. Pup tried to stand, but the pain pulled him down, into a dark and dreamless sleep.

Pup woke to the rattle of chains and dogs baying and barking. But these weren't the lost, lonely and bored barks of Dogsdoom, these were angry defensive barks, full of aggression and fear. He opened his eyes and tried to get to his feet. Everything hurt. His face was swollen, and his ears burned where they had been ripped to shreds.

He looked around him. He was in a big open yard. There were dogs chained to long wires so that the dogs could run up and down but not reach each other. He could smell the scents of the city, of car fumes and traffic, and he caught the scent of the river drifting on the breeze from the east. Above the walls surrounding the yard he could see a vast concrete bridge that thundered with fast lorries and cars.

The Master was walking between the dogs, throwing food onto the ground. There were all sorts of dogs, all muscled and strong. They greeted the Master with wagging tails and affection.

Thor took a marrow bone from the Master and settled down to chew it. He looked across at Pup. 'You survived the night.'

Pup licked at the angry wounds on his legs that Thor had inflicted. 'Why do you show him any favour?' growled Pup.

'He is our master,' said Thor. 'Did your mother not tell you the story of the Great Sky Wolf? Man is our master.'

'No,' said Pup. 'We are his equal. It is a bond of friendship.'

Thor curled his lip. 'You believe that, do you? The Great Sky Wolf turned his back on us. We are dogs, servants of the Great Hunter, Orion. We were put up in the sky to serve Him. Man chooses us. We do not choose him. Man is our master.'

'He is no master of mine,' growled Pup, but his thoughts felt confused. He tried to remember Saffy's story. What had Saffy said about the Great Sky Wolf? How could Thor's version of the story be so different? Which was the true story? He turned to Thor. 'Our bond with man is not one of servitude, it is of love. We give our heart to man and our soul to the Great Wolf in the sky.'

Thor crunched on the bone. 'Then you're a fool. And probably a dead one. If you don't fight, you'll die.'

'Why does the Master make us fight each other?' asked Pup.

'So that he can be powerful among men,' said Thor.

'Fools!' said a voice above him.

Pup turned around. High on the wall was a cat, a thin, lithe tabby. She sat perfectly still, twitching the end of her tail.

Thor growled but turned his back on her.

The cat leaped down from the wall and the nearest dog lunged at her, snapping and snarling, straining at the end of its chain to get her, but she remained a whisker out of reach.

'All dogs are fools,' she said, walking close to Pup. She turned her green eyes on him. 'They are savage servants of man.'

Pup just stared at her. He'd never been so close to a cat before. He'd seen them in the distance and Clown had loved to chase them, but had often come back with a scratched nose.

The cat sauntered up to him. 'You're new.'

Pup tried to back away but yelped at the pain in his leg.

She looked at his tattered ears. 'Dogs are such savages,' she said. 'You rely on brute force. You should try to be more cat,' she purred.

'What do you mean?' said Pup.

The cat curled her paw to unsheathe a set of fine sharp claws. 'Maybe I'll show you one day.'

'Ignore her,' growled Thor. 'There is nothing useful to be learned from a cat. She is jealous that man loves us.'

The cat turned and walked towards Thor, her tail high in the air. 'Then why is it that I share the warmth of his fire while you shiver out here in the cold?'

Thor sprang at her, straining at the end of his chain.

The cat licked her paw and yawned. 'Just a brute,' she purred. 'And no brains.'

Pup watched her jump up onto the wall again and walk away towards the brick house at the far end. She leaped lightly through an open window and disappeared inside.

Pup watched her go. Maybe there were things that dogs could learn from cats after all.

*

Pup's wounds took a long time to heal, but as the days lengthened, he felt stronger with the spring sun on his fur. The Master gave him raw meat and bones to chew and Pup could feel the weight come back to his body. The Master also trained him, but instead of the runs he had done with Max, the Master tied him up to a treadmill and made him run for hours. Pup didn't mind. He loved to run. It cleared his mind from all other thoughts, leaving him numb, letting him exist without feeling anything at all. The Master also made him pull tug-of-war to strengthen his jaws. And as the months rolled through the summer to another winter, Pup felt stronger than he'd ever been before.

Even Thor looked warily at him now. 'The Master will think you are ready soon.'

'Ready?'

'Yes,' grumbled Thor. 'Ready to fight.'

Pup rested his head on his paws. 'I'm not fighting at his will.'

'You'll have to, to stay alive,' said Thor.

And winter passed into another spring, and the Master felt Pup's muscles and looked at his teeth. 'Time to see what you're made of.'

Pup was put in the van and taken with three other dogs across bumpy roads to the barn in the green land beyond the city. Pup recognized the railings set in a circle and the dirt floor. Bile rose in his throat at the memory.

The Master led him into the ring and another dog was released too. It was a bulky dog, smaller than him but well-muscled. It went into a snarling frenzy and launched at

Pup, but Pup leaped out of the way. The men were leering, their faces red with the excitement of seeing dogs rip each other apart. Pup felt anger rush through him. Rex had been right. Men had no love of dogs. They used them for their own fun. There was no sacred bond.

Pup flew at the men, his body slamming into the wire mesh, sending those near to him hooting and whooping. They clapped and jeered, bashing the railings with their hands, but Pup couldn't reach them. The other dog bit hard onto Pup's leg, and Pup turned all the fury he felt at man onto the dog, biting it and shaking it like a rat. He didn't stop until the dog crawled away from him along the ground and would not fight back. The men spurred on the dogs to fight, but the terrier was too scared, and Pup did not want to fight him again. The anger inside him raged, but he felt shame too. He had done his Master's bidding, to fight another dog to defeat or death.

That night the Master gave Pup a piece of prime steak.

Thor looked across. 'Enjoy it while you can. Each fight will get harder and the dogs bigger.'

'How many dogs have you fought?' asked Pup.

'I can't remember now,' said Thor. 'But I remember the first one.'

'Did you win?' said Pup.

'No, I was like you. Almost left for dead,' said Thor.

Pup finished his steak and licked his lips. 'Will the Master make us fight each other again?'

'No chance,' said Thor. 'He doesn't want his own dogs to injure each other. We are too valuable to him now.'

Thor was right.

The Master took Pup to different fights, where he had to fight for his life.

The venues changed, but they always smelled of bravado and fear.

At each fight, Pup fought only if he was attacked. Then he fought with all his ferocity and power. He let his mind lose itself in the frenzy of the attack, imagining he was tearing the flesh of the Master or the men who goaded and shouted at the dogs.

Word spread that the Master had the two most powerful dogs, Thor and The Werewolf. He walked with them by his side, both muzzled and growling at anyone and any dog.

Pup hated men. Rex had been right. They were all the same in the end. The story of the Great Sky Wolf was just a story. It was a story to chain dogs into loyalty to man. Sirius had betrayed dogs to leave them at the mercy of man.

It was man's world. Dogs had no control of their own lives. Pup envied the wolves, wild and free to live as a pack.

They had not sacrificed their freedom.

Pup was trapped.

He was alive until his next fight.

It was the only way to survive.

He was a fighting dog now.

Chapter 30
THOR'S DOWNFALL

ANOTHER YEAR CAME AND WENT. Pup too lost count of the number of fights. But he never fought with dogs that had been stolen from homes and families. These dogs came, bewildered and whimpering, away from a world of love to a world of cruelty. They were used to train the younger fighting dogs to get a taste for blood. Pup turned his back on them all.

As another summer wore on, Pup liked to curl up and watch the stars as they crossed the sky. In early summer the dog star, Sirius, disappeared from the night sky and slept below the western horizon. Pup wanted to run towards the place where Sirius was sleeping, towards the place Saffy had told them about, to the long white sand where the ocean meets the sky at the end of the world. He often tried to remember the face of his boy, but he sometimes couldn't picture him at all. The memory of him seemed so long distant, almost like a dream he couldn't quite recall. Maybe it was best that way. Sometimes he tried to forget. But one night his boy came to him in his dreams, unreachable at the end of his chain, calling to Pup to join him. Pup woke up, his heart pounding, and he was gasping for breath.

'You howl in your dreams,' said Thor. 'Who are you calling to?'

Pup shook himself. Who was he howling to? His boy? Frenchi? Saffy and Rex? For baby Lena? Maybe he was howling for the life he had lost.

'Have you ever had a human who loved you?' said Pup.

Thor put his big head in his paws. 'No.'

'Not one?' said Pup.

Thor thought hard. 'There was a child once. When I was a small pup. We played, I think.' He snapped at a buzzing fly. 'But I was taken away after that.'

'Don't you want to escape and get away?' said Pup.

'And go where?' said Thor. 'With who? Where would I stay? What would I eat?'

'We could go together,' said Pup.

Thor stared at him. 'There is no other life for a dog like you or me. And you're only alive until your next fight.'

Pup closed his eyes and tried to remember the shape of his boy. Thor was right. He was a fighting dog now, wary and battle-scarred. All dogs except for Thor feared him. Humans were wary of him. If he escaped, there would be nowhere to go. He would always be on the run.

Pup and Thor were the Master's favourites. They had steak and big fresh marrow bones. They fought battles and were paraded about as trophies.

Then one afternoon, the Master came to collect Thor. 'We have the fight of our lives tonight, Thor,' he said, giving the dog another piece of steak. 'There's a new dog in town. And I've wagered a lot of money on this fight.'

Pup watched Thor and two other dogs being loaded into the van, but he wasn't chosen tonight.

Thor was intimidating in size and voice. Even when he leaped into the van, his weight made the van tilt to the side. But that summer evening, when the van returned, the Master opened the doors and the two terriers jumped out. Then he slammed the doors closed and Thor was nowhere to be seen. The Master chained the two terriers up, kicking at one of them, sending it scuttling away. He swore and kicked the other dog before he stormed into his house.

Pup waited until the dogs had settled. 'Where's Thor?'

The other dog looked warily at Pup. 'Thor is dead.'

'Dead?' said Pup. He remembered Thor's words. *You're only alive until your next fight.*

The other dog shivered. 'There's another dog out there. He's bigger and fiercer. Thor had no chance.'

'Thor is dead?' repeated Pup.

'He put up a good fight,' said the dog. 'But the other dog was much stronger. I've never seen a dog like it. He was savage.'

'What did he look like?' asked Pup.

'Huge one,' said the dog. 'A white one.'

Pup shuddered. 'Did he have a name?'

The dog tucked his tail beneath his legs at the memory. 'He said his name is Fang.'

Chapter 31
FANG

THE MASTER DIDN'T TAKE ANY dogs out for several months. He acquired new dogs and fed them up. He trained them harder, running them until they fell exhausted to the ground. He gave them bones to crunch to strengthen their jaws.

The cat watched from a distance, or sometimes walked between them, teasing them with her presence.

'Your master builds you up, yet you will always lose against a bigger, stronger dog,' she said to Pup.

'It's how we survive,' said Pup. 'Whoever is strongest wins.'

'Cats use brains to survive,' said the cat. She looked at Pup's scars. 'Such brutality. Such barbarism, pulling each other apart.' She disappeared for a while and then came back carrying a huge dead rat in her mouth. The rat was almost as big as she was. She dumped it near Pup.

'Look, not a scratch or a scar. Yet this rat is as big as me and fearsome too,' said the cat. 'Rats put up good fight.'

Pup sniffed at it. Its body was still warm, yet there were no tooth marks or no blood. 'How?' asked Pup.

The cat blinked and looked at Pup. 'We cats do not maul our prey. We bite the throat so our prey cannot breathe. It's swift and painless. And clean.'

Pup watched her leave with the rat and felt jealous of her freedom. Cats had worked out humans, he thought. They took humans' food, shelter and affection yet were not servants to them. They were a law unto themselves.

As the dogs' training continued, Pup thought of the dog named Fang who had killed Thor. Was it the same dog, the leader of the Sewer Dogs who Rex had saved him from all those years ago? Had Fang been caught and brought into this world too? Pup knew he was big enough and fierce enough to survive in this world. Ruthless enough too.

It wasn't until the darkening days of early winter that Pup got to find out. The air was scented with woodsmoke from bonfires. The nights came so cold that the Master even laid straw for the dogs and gave them wooden packing cases as kennels to sleep in. Water on the ground turned to ice.

One night, the Master loaded Pup in the van and took him further into the city. 'You'll have to finish what Thor started,' said the Master. 'I'm not taking back another dead dog tonight.'

The Master pulled up near the edge of the city beside a derelict building. The weeds had taken over. The only signs of humans were lights from deep in the building and a man smoking in the shadows, the red end of his cigarette glowing as he inhaled. Pup could hear the rumble of trains, but no familiar scents, except for the smell of a river. It smelled like the same river that had flowed near the Railway Den.

The Master led Pup inside the building. It was lit by a flickering strobe light that seemed to make the air in the building even colder. It was a busy gathering. Pup was aware of dogs and men in the shadows, all watchful of each other. In the centre of the building was the fighting ring. This time it was made out of a plywood fence.

The air was clouded with smoke, but Pup could see a white dog on the other side of the room. It was huge and well-muscled.

It was Fang, the leader of the Sewer Dogs.

He would have to fight Fang tonight.

The man who held Fang was young. He had skinny jeans and quick sharp eyes, and even the people around him kept their distance. He stood up and walked across the room and placed Fang inside the ring, holding onto his collar. Men began to gather around. Someone shouted and lifted another dog into the ring. Pup heard other men bursting into laughter. This must be a bait dog, Pup thought, just to show the strength of Fang and how quickly he could kill. It would be a weak dog with no fight in it. It would be pitiful. Pup had no desire to watch it die.

Pup lay down at the Master's feet and tried to ignore the sound of Fang's baying for blood. But another sound made Pup sit up. From inside the ring came a snorting and snuffling, and a huffing and a puffing. It was a sound he recognized. The men were still laughing and pointing at the dog in the ring.

Then Pup could hear the dog's voice imploring Fang.

'Look now, let's just talk about this, shall we . . . ?'

Pup knew that voice. He knew who was making the snuffling grunts. 'Frenchi?' he barked. 'Frenchi . . . Frenchi . . . Frenchi!'

Pup jumped forward, pulling the lead out of the Master's hand. He leaped into the ring. 'Frenchi!'

The squat French bulldog looked up. He snuffed the air

and peered at the big dog facing him. 'Pup! Is that you? Is that really you?'

'It's me, Frenchi, it's me, it's me, it's me!' barked Pup, his tail wagging so hard he couldn't stop.

Fang strained against the skinny man's hold on his collar. He snarled at Pup and Frenchi. 'Well, if it isn't the dogs from the Railway Den.' He stared at them both. 'I'll take you both down. I've waited for this moment.'

Pup spun around to face him, showing all his teeth and snarling back.

The skinny man laughed. 'Looks like your dog wants to fight over this mutt.'

The Master looked in the ring. Both Fang and Pup were big powerful dogs, but Fang was the heavier, stronger dog.

'The Werewolf will tear your dog apart,' said the Master.

'How much?' said the skinny man. 'How much d'you want to bet?'

'Two thousand,' said the Master.

'Five thousand,' said the skinny man.

The Master nodded his head and shook hands, and the skinny man unclipped Fang from the lead.

'Stay behind me, Frenchi,' said Pup.

Fang growled. 'Where's that big dog to save you now? What happened to him? Dogsdoom, I reckon. And we all know what happens to Forbiddens.'

Pup snarled back. 'Back off.'

'I haven't lost a fight yet,' said Fang.

'You did,' growled Pup. 'You lost to Rex and you're going to lose to me too.'

Fang launched forward, a blur of weight and speed. Pup tried to dodge but he was knocked off his feet as Fang's head butted his chest. Then Fang was on him, pinning him down, biting and snarling. Pup was crushed beneath him, unable to move. He bit down onto Fang's ear and Fang yowled in pain, letting Pup struggle free. But then Fang launched on him again, pushing him into the dirt. Pup knew he could never beat Fang like this. Fang was heavier and more powerful.

He thought of the cat: *use your brains to survive.*

Pup struggled free again and backed away, tail tucked in submission.

'A coward,' growled Fang, lunging for the kill.

As Fang leaped, Pup slid beneath him, knocking him off his feet, and then he twisted to spin on top of him. Before Fang could stop him, Pup clamped his jaws on Fang's throat, so hard that Fang couldn't breathe.

Fang thrashed with his feet and he tried to shake Pup off, but he couldn't. He threw himself against the wooden walls of the ring, splitting them and breaking them, but Pup hung on as the two big dogs tumbled out of the ring. The humans were cheering and jeering at the frenzy. Fang couldn't turn his head to bite, and as Pup held tight, his jaws crushing Fang's throat, Fang became limp, struggling to breathe, spittle flying from his mouth. The noise of the men yelling and chanting filled Pup's head. It wasn't until he felt Frenchi tugging at him that he stopped.

'Let him go, Pup,' urged Frenchi.

Pup let go, and Fang lay gasping on the ground.

'Come on,' said Pup, 'follow me.' He bared his teeth at

any human that blocked their path and led Frenchi away, following the draught of fresh air that promised to lead outside.

The Master stood in front of him, but rage still ran through Pup's blood. He leaped at the Master, pushing him down and biting at his hands and face until the Master curled up in a ball, and screamed for help.

'Run!' yelled Frenchi. 'Let's get out of here.'

Frenchi ran into the shadows while other people tried to corner Pup, but Pup was wild with rage. He lunged at anyone who came near, then bounded into the darkness after Frenchi.

'This way,' said Frenchi. 'I smell fresh air.'

They reached a metal door where cool air was blowing beneath the gap at the floor.

Behind them came shouts and running footsteps.

'We tried,' said Frenchi. He scrabbled at the ground beneath the door, trying to dig his way through. 'So near, yet so far.'

But Pup knew all about doors. He rose up on his hind legs and pulled the handle down.

The door swung wide open.

And Pup and Frenchi escaped into the night.

Chapter 32
LEE

'THIS WAY,' SAID FRENCHI. HE huffed and puffed and Pup could see that he was much slower than he had been before.

The sound of footsteps came after them.

'I'll fight them off,' said Pup.

Frenchi looked behind. 'There are too many. We need to be invisible, remember?' He crawled beneath a parked van, and Pup crawled on his belly after him. The spreading beam from a security light lit the road, and Pup could see the silhouettes of men spill out from the building. He could see the Master too, looking up and down, and his feet pacing alongside the van. But the road was empty. The Master slammed his hand down on the bonnet of the van and cursed into the night.

'Just wait,' whispered Frenchi. 'Don't move.'

Pup and Frenchi watched the men walk back into the building, then Frenchi scrambled out. 'Come on,' he said. 'Let's get away from here.'

'Where are we going?' asked Pup.

Frenchi sniffed the night air. 'I don't know this place, but I can smell the river. We'll follow the river into the city. We'll be safe there.'

Frenchi was slow and needed to stop often. His breathing was laboured and he was limping too. The sore on his worry-paw was much bigger, the edges angry and red.

Frenchi wanted to know all about Pup, and so Pup told him. Many winters had passed since he had seen Frenchi, and he had grown strong while Frenchi had grown old. Frenchi was stiff and the black markings on his face were peppered with white hairs of old age. Pup told him about Dogsdoom, and about Saffy and about Rex. He told him about Max and Zofia and baby Lena. But Pup couldn't bring himself to tell Frenchi about meeting his boy. The memory was too painful, too raw. It was a brief moment that had been stolen from him. He had to put it somewhere he couldn't reach. He had to forget.

Frenchi stopped to have a rest when they reached the river. He looked up at the stars beyond the thinning clouds. 'Rex was a true friend,' he said. 'Loyal and true. He didn't deserve to die like that.'

'He was right about man,' growled Pup.

Frenchi looked up at him. 'Surely you don't mean that, Pup. Don't forget the sacred bond . . .'

'There is no sacred bond,' growled Pup. 'It's a lie. I've seen man for what he is. I have no trust in him.'

Frenchi got up and shook himself. 'Come on, Pup. I think you're wrong. I want you to meet someone.'

Pup didn't move. 'Who? A human?'

Frenchi began walking upriver towards the glowing skyline of the city. 'Yes, a human.'

'I thought it would be just you and me,' said Pup. 'I'm not going near any human.'

'I have to go back to him,' said Frenchi.

Pup stopped. 'What about us? I want you to be with me.'

Frenchi turned around. 'It will always be us,' said Frenchi. 'You might want my friendship, but you are grown now and can look after yourself. You don't need me any more. But this human needs me. Come with me, Pup, then decide.'

Pup watched Frenchi trot away, then followed at a distance. He didn't want to live with humans again, or even be near them. They couldn't be trusted. They were either nasty, or they let you down, or they broke your heart.

A pale dawn was breaking over the city. Mist hung over the river, reaching the edges of the riverbank where the path was overgrown with weeds and wide puddles of oily water. The dark spaces beneath bridges that ran over the river echoed with the morning traffic. Frenchi trotted on until he reached a wide bridge carrying a railway over the river. Rubbish had been tipped beneath. There were piles of tyres and boxes, and an old fridge. Trains rumbled overhead, reminding Pup of the Railway Den.

Frenchi stopped and sniffed the air.

Pup stopped too and sniffed. There were all sorts of smells mixed together: train fumes, sewage, rats, and human scent. Frenchi trotted up to the pile of rubbish and began digging at it with his feet. Pup sniffed the air again. He could smell a human very close but couldn't see him. Then a pile of cardboard shifted and moved, and a head poked out.

It was a man with matted hair and wiry beard. He had a fresh cut below one eye and a bruise across half of his face. He held out his hand to Frenchi. 'Hello, my friend. Patch, is that you?'

'Uff!' barked Frenchi. He frantically wagged the stub of his tail and shuffled toward the man.

The man crawled out of his shelter and pulled Frenchi into his arms and hugged him. 'Patch! My little friend, I thought you were lost for good,' he said. He looked Frenchi all over. 'And you're OK. Those men did me in good and proper when they took you.' He ran his fingers around the edge of the bruise. 'How did you escape, little friend?'

Frenchi wriggled out of the man's arms and trotted over to Pup. 'Uff!' he barked. He turned to Pup. 'This is Lee. He's looked after me since we left the Railway Den.'

Pup stayed in the shadows and stared at Lee. The man's face was gaunt, and despite looking young, he had wrinkled skin and his eyes were tinged with yellow.

Lee looked back and smiled, showing a row of broken teeth. 'So you've found yourself a friend,' he said. He held out his hand but Pup growled softly.

'I don't blame you, mate,' said Lee. 'Don't trust no one, do you? But if you're a friend of Patch, then you're a friend of mine.' He reached into his bag to pull out a piece of bread and gave some to Frenchi and then threw some to Pup.

'Eat,' said Frenchi. 'We never know where the next meal is coming from.'

'Is this where Lee lives?' asked Pup.

'We live anywhere and everywhere,' said Frenchi. 'We don't stay in the same place too long. This place was good until those men took me.'

Lee shuffled to his feet and began gathering a few of his belongings. He rolled up his blanket and stuffed it into his bag. 'We'd best get going,' he said. 'Don't want those men to come back and find us.' He hugged Frenchi again.

'Good to see you, mate. Good to see you. Didn't think I would.'

'Uff,' said Frenchi.

Lee turned to Pup. 'You can come too, if you want.'

Pup stayed in the shadows and padded along behind them. Pup noticed that Lee walked with a limp too, like Frenchi. As the sun rose higher in the sky, they followed Lee across to the sunlit side of the river to warm themselves in the weak winter sun. In the afternoon, the clouds gathered and cold drizzle started to fall, and Lee led Frenchi and Pup beneath a piece of loose fencing into a disused garage site. Around the back of the building there was an old metal drum that Lee began to fill with dry paper from his bag. He scoured the site for pieces of plywood and cardboard.

'Lee doesn't get a fire going often,' said Frenchi. 'It's a bit risky see, with the flames. Sometimes other street folk come and sit and chat, but other times the police come and move us along. Sometimes it's street gangs that come and they aren't so nice.'

Pup watched as Lee filled the metal drum and lit a match. The flames licked up the sides, and Lee kept feeding fuel to keep it going. Soon it settled down to a warm glow, and Lee wrapped his blanket around himself and Frenchi. The rain had stopped, but a chill wind blew and Pup was keen to feel the warmth of the fire. He sidled nearer until he could feel the heat on his skin.

Lee threw some more bread to Pup. 'You've seen a few fights, haven't you, boy?' he said, looking at Pup's ripped and torn ears and the scars on his body. 'How did you get to be on the streets, eh?'

Pup whined.

Lee pulled a bottle from his pocket and unscrewed the lid. He took a swig and stared into the fire. 'Well, I guess it can happen to anyone. Never thought it would be me.' He threw a strip of old carpet onto the fire and watched black smoke billow up, and the shadows leap and dance. 'I had it all once,' he said. 'I had a house, food on the table and a job.' He took another swig from the bottle. 'I had a wife and baby son. Angela and Jack.'

Pup moved a little closer to the fire.

Frenchi curled up in Lee's lap and closed his eyes.

But Lee was lost in his memory, and now he had another soul to listen to his story. 'It was Christmas Eve,' he said to Pup. 'Angela had been to see her mother with Jack. My Angela, with her raven hair and ocean eyes. I had the music playing and the wine ready. Presents were under the tree, and there was a plate of mince pies for Father Christmas by the chimney. It was Jack's first Christmas. I was waiting for them.' He took a glug of drink. 'But they never came home. A drink-driver ploughed into their car. And they were gone. My world fell apart after that.'

Lee upended the bottle and gulped the liquid down, staring into the flames. 'My Angela, with her raven hair and ocean eyes,' he said again. 'And the most precious thing I have ever held in my arms, my sweet baby Jack.'

'It's his fire-water,' said Frenchi to Pup. 'To remember and to forget.'

Pup watched Lee lie down on the hard ground, pulling the blanket over him and Frenchi. A soft rain started to fall, and Pup curled up near the fire, listening to the hiss of raindrops on the hot embers. He lay awake listening to Frenchi's snuffling snores. But somehow, they didn't comfort him this time. Somehow, they made him feel even more alone. Before, when he was a pup, he'd thought Frenchi could protect him from all harm and keep him safe, but now that he was older he saw that his brave, loyal Frenchi was doing all he could just to survive. The world was big and wide and lonely. Frenchi had found Lee, and they had clung to each other in a world that had turned its back on them both.

As the rain stopped, the clouds cleared in the sky. Pup looked for the dog star to find hope in the stories that Saffy had told. But the stars blinked back at him with a cold white light, and he found no comfort there. The old stories were just stories, he thought, to give hope when there was no hope in the real world to be found.

Chapter 33
SILENT NIGHT

THE NIGHTS BECAME COLDER, AND Pup stayed with Lee and Frenchi. Sometimes Lee would sleep on a park bench, sometimes in a doorway or beneath an underpass. Some nights, Lee and Frenchi stayed in a hostel for other humans who lived on the streets. Lee was only allowed one dog, and so on those nights Pup would find his own shelter or he would just run through the city.

Some days Pup would sit with Lee and Frenchi on the hard ground and watch people passing by. Lee often held Frenchi on his lap, wrapping him in his blanket to keep him warm. Frenchi's snuffles were worse on cold days, and sometimes he struggled to breathe, his wide tongue hanging out, gulping the air. Sometimes people stopped to crouch down and stroke Frenchi, but they never wanted to touch Pup. Some gave money and food, but most passed by, as if they weren't even there. As winter deepened and Christmas approached, the streets were strung with coloured lights, and the pavements were crowded with shoppers. The smell of roasting chestnuts filled the air and the store fronts sparkled with bright goods.

Lee loved to hear people sing. He often took Frenchi and Pup to the park or a street corner to listen to carol singers. On Christmas Eve, as the air sparkled with ice, he led them into a church to the pews at the back. The minister had cast an eye on both dogs, but when he saw Frenchi sitting quietly on Lee's lap, and Pup lying near his feet, he said nothing.

Pup listened to the minister tell a story of a baby boy sent to save the world. Humans had their stories too, thought Pup. Maybe their stories gave them hope when there seemed none to be found.

The humans began to sing together, the same song. Lee's voice joined them, tears falling down his face. Pup felt the sound fill his chest. He wanted to howl with them. But this was their song, their story, so he stayed quiet and curled up at Lee's feet. Maybe humans sang, just as wolves howled, to tell their stories and bind them to each other. Maybe it was a way of saying, *Hear me. I am here. I am here, for you.*

Lee swaddled Frenchi in his blanket and held him against his chest, rocking him in his arms as he sang with the music, the words rising up to the rafters;

Silent night, holy night.
All is calm, all is bright,
Round yon virgin, Mother and Child,
Holy infant so tender and mild,
Sleep in heavenly peace.
Sleep in heavenly peace.

Lee left the service before the end and shuffled out into the night. The night had become colder and big soft flakes of snow began to fall. He held out his hand, one snowflake coming to rest on his glove. 'Snow, at Christmas,' he said with a smile. 'Just imagine that.'

He asked at a hostel for a bed, but the hostel was full. He tapped his pocket, feeling the full bottle of fire-water he had to see him through the night. He stopped at a shop front, took several glugs from his bottle and lay down on a dry patch of ground. It was Christmas Eve and the shops would be closed the next day. There would be nobody to disturb him. No one to move him on. Lee lay with his back to the world and pulled his blanket over him.

'It's too cold here,' said Pup. 'It's going to get colder, I can feel it.'

Frenchi wriggled under the blanket. 'There's no room for you here. Go and find somewhere warm tonight and come back tomorrow.'

'It's too cold for you too,' said Pup. 'Rain is coming. Lee has to move.'

Frenchi pushed his nose against Lee, but Lee just grunted. 'He's had too much fire-water. He can't go far.'

'Then come with me,' said Pup.

I can't leave him,' said Frenchi. 'I am all he has.'

'Frenchi . . .'

'Pup, there is a story I haven't told you,' said Frenchi. 'I have been too ashamed to tell it. Only Saffy knew. When I was abandoned in Dead Dog Alley, one of the street sleepers looked after me. I went with him everywhere. But one night it was bitter cold, like tonight, and I left him to go and find somewhere warm. When I returned he wasn't there, and I never saw him again. I wasn't there for him when he needed me. I tried to make it up, by rescuing "lost souls", as Saffy put it. But I couldn't rescue him. So I'll stay with Lee and keep him warm. Because I can't bear the thought of him being alone. I don't want my heart broken again.'

'Then I'll stay with you,' said Pup.

'There's no room under this blanket for you,' said Frenchi.

'Come with me,' said Pup. He tried to paw his friend to pull him out.

But Frenchi bared his teeth and growled. 'Do as I ask, Pup.' He softened when Pup backed away. 'Besides, I'm tired too, Pup. Look at me. I can't walk far these days. Lee has to carry me. Come back tomorrow and bring breakfast. Find something for us to eat. Christmas is a time of plenty.'

Pup whined and walked away. When he reached the end of the street he turned and could see that Frenchi had crawled under the blanket with Lee. Man and his faithful dog, sleeping side by side.

Pup padded through the park to the top of the hill to look at the Christmas moon. It was past midnight and the streets were empty. People were at home tucked up in their beds. Pup stopped at the top of the hill. His warm breath misted in the frosty air.

It was a silent night. A holy night.

All was calm.

And all was bright.

The clouds had cleared to show the star-scattered sky. A deep unexplained sadness filled Pup's soul. And as the world turned, Pup watched the constellations of Orion and his dog sink down together below the southwestern horizon, falling into celestial sleep. Man, and his faithful dog, resting in heavenly peace.

The Boy

The boy watches the snow falling past his window on Christmas Eve. He is now a young man of eighteen years. He has walked away from that house full of anger and has decided his own future. He is learning his trade as a carpenter and rents a room from a lady who lives by the canal on the green fringes of the city.

It is safe. It is quiet. For now, it is home.

He sits in his room, listening to carols drifting up from the TV in the kitchen below. In his hand he holds a small piece of wood that he has carved and shaped into a small wooden dog. He uses a fine chisel to mark the lines of fur. He carves the memory while fine flakes of sawdust drift down like snow.

He has never stopped searching for Pup. He has roamed the city and walked the kennelled corridors of the rescue centres, but with every passing year, hopes of finding him fade. He wonders if he just has to accept that Pup is gone, that he will never see him again.

He looks up at the Christmas moon.

He thinks, maybe it is enough to know he was loved.

Love is a gift, he thinks. The greatest gift of all.

Chapter 34
NO DOG
AT ALL

Pup walked the whole night.

Dark clouds rolled over the city again and a cold sleety rain fell. He walked and walked until the first slivers of dawn began to brighten the sky. He stopped to take a short rest beside a vent next to hotel kitchens that blasted out hot stuffy air. He curled up, alone, tucking his nose into his fur, and before he knew it, he fell into a deep and troubled sleep.

He dreamed he was back in Dead Dog Alley, but this time there were lots of different alleyways leading off into the darkness, and however hard he searched, he just couldn't find Frenchi.

He woke to the sound of a chef emptying food in the bins of the hotel. He shook himself and peered out. A cold winter sun had already risen above the skyline and washed colour out of the day. Pup had slept longer than he had meant to and worried that Frenchi and Lee would be waiting for their breakfast and wondering where he was. Pup kept in the shadows until the chef had gone back inside the kitchens, then he rummaged in the bin for some food. He found half a chicken with meat still on the bones and set off to find his friend. Most of the snow had been washed away but some lay in dirty black piles on the pavement. A bitter wind funnelled down the road and drove deep into his thick fur, and the salty grit worked its way between his toes and stung his sore paws.

He passed houses where the smell of roasting Christmas dinner drifted out onto the street. He caught glimpses of people inside warm houses, sitting together, watching TV and playing games. A cat in a window stared at him, her tail puffed up as if to say, *I see you*. At another house he stopped to watch two young children kicking a new football in a driveway. A dog ran up to the gate, barking furiously at him. Pup heard someone coming so he turned and trotted away, not wanting to be seen. He let himself wonder if he and Frenchi could have been taken in with a family together, if they could have slept by a fire and played in a garden. Seeing other families and their dogs made Pup feel even more alone. He wanted to be with Frenchi more than ever.

He broke into a hurried trot and headed back into the centre of the city.

The Christmas lights illuminated empty streets and reflected from the puddles. The shops were closed, and many had steel shutters pulled down. Further ahead, Pup could see Frenchi and Lee curled up where he'd left them, and he trotted faster to be with them, keen to get out of the wind. But as Pup drew close, he could sense something was wrong. Lee was still, too still. His lips were blue and there was no heat coming from him. There was no breath misting the cold air.

Pup slowed to a walk and took a step closer.

He couldn't hear Frenchi's snuffling snores.

'Frenchi?' said Pup. He dropped the chicken and pawed the blanket, pulling it away to see Frenchi curled up with Lee. But Frenchi was cold too.

'Frenchi?' whined Pup, pawing at his friend. 'Wake up.'

But Frenchi would never wake up. He had been brave and true to the very end.

Pup felt the loss take hold of him. He had lost everything he had ever known or loved. He tried to wriggle beside Frenchi, but there was no thump, thump, thump of the dog's heart. There were no comforting rumbling and snuffling snores.

Frenchi, brave loyal Frenchi, was dead.

He had gone somewhere that Pup couldn't follow. Pup sat next to him and lifted back his head and howled. He howled for the world to hear. He howled for the Great Sky Wolf to come and take Frenchi's soul away.

He howled because it was the only thing he could do.

Pup's howls brought two nurses who were walking back from their night shift at a hospital. One bent down to lift the blanket, while the other kept a watchful eye on Pup.

'Oh my,' one whispered. 'So sad. Poor things.'

The other nurse called on her phone and they waited for an ambulance to arrive to take Lee away.

Pup tried to squeeze himself next to his friend and he licked Frenchi's cold ears. When the ambulance arrived Pup wouldn't let them take Lee. If they took Lee, they would take Frenchi. And if they took Frenchi, Pup wouldn't have anyone in the world.

Pup stood in front of Frenchi and Lee, his hackles raised and a growl rumbling in his throat. He would guard Frenchi's body. He would stay here with him for ever.

The paramedics waited until a police car and a white van arrived. Pup knew the smell of the white van too well.

It was the van from Dogsdoom.

When the Snatchers approached, he snarled at them, and when they looped the rope over his neck he fought, twisting and turning and trying to bite them. He wanted to stay here, with Frenchi. They pinned him down on the freezing ground and held him, his face pressed into a pool of dirty water. He watched the paramedics lift Lee into the waiting ambulance, and then police officers wrapped Frenchi in Lee's blanket and carried him away.

Frenchi was gone, and now Pup was alone.

There was nothing left to fight for any more. Even if he could escape, there was nowhere to go and there was nowhere to run.

He remembered Frenchi's words from years ago. *A dog on his own is no dog at all.*

Pup stopped struggling.

All the fight went from him.

He closed his eyes and let the Snatchers pull a muzzle over his nose. He didn't even try to stand. He let them lift him into the van.

He was going back to Dogsdoom, but he knew that this time there would be no training sessions with the Aprons, and no humans to come and choose him.

He was a biter now, a danger to man.

There would be only one way out.

Through the Door of No Return.

Chapter 35
ONE, TWO AND
NO MORE

PUP DIDN'T STRUGGLE WHEN THEY dragged him out of the van. He let them carry him to an inspection room where one of the Needles examined him. When the Needle tried to take off his muzzle to look inside his mouth, he growled, and so the Needles gave him an injection to make him feel sleepy before they could check his mouth and teeth. Then the Aprons carried him on a stretcher to a kennel, where they lay him on the hard, concrete floor, removed his muzzle and left him alone where he sank into a deep and anxious sleep.

Pup woke to the barking of other dogs and the clanging of doors and bowls at feeding time. He sat up, swaying and feeling still groggy and sleepy. He recognized the row of kennels from before. He looked across at Roly's kennel, but a different dog was in its place. Pup tried to remember how many winters had passed since he had been in Dogsdoom. The smells and noise seemed more intense than before.

An Apron pushed a bowl of food into his kennel and stepped back, shutting the door. Pup growled at her, a low warning growl. He wanted nothing to do with humans any more. Rex had been right. They always let you down in the end.

Pup stared at his food, but slumped back down to the floor. He didn't notice a dog in the neighbouring kennel sniffing through the bars.

'Pup, is that you?'

Pup turned and blinked. An old collie was watching him.

'One, two . . .' it said. 'One, two . . .'

'Merle?' said Pup, sitting up.

'Pup, it *is* you,' said Merle. She wagged her tail and tried to push her nose through the bars. 'I thought you were a night-shadow.'

'A night-shadow?' said Pup.

'They haunt my sleep. They run past me and I can't stop counting them. The numbers never end. They drive me mad. They never end.' She looked at Pup's shredded ears and the scars on his face. 'Oh, Pup, what happened to you?'

Pup slunk back into the shadows. He didn't want to talk.

'What about the others?' said Merle.

'Frenchi and Rex are gone,' said Pup. 'Saffy found a home with people.'

'It's just us, then,' said Merle. 'Clown died.' She whined and pressed her head against the bars. 'He crossed the road without looking. He didn't see the car. You know Clown. Too fast, too full of life.'

'Poor Clown,' said Pup.

'One, two and no more,' whined Merle.

Pup curled himself up in the corner. He didn't want to think about Clown or Frenchi or Rex or Saffy or Reynard or Lady Fifi.

'The Lookers come tomorrow,' said Merle. 'I've been here for two winters, but there's a lady coming to take me with her soon. Maybe she can take you too?'

'Rex was right about humans,' growled Pup. 'I don't trust them any more.'

271

Merle just stared at him. 'You can't mean that. What about the bond?'

Pup curled his lip. 'There is no bond. I've seen what men are capable of. I've seen what they can do.'

'There will be someone for you,' said Merle. 'Remember what Saffy used to say.'

'I don't want anyone,' said Pup. 'Humans always let you down.'

Merle pawed the bars between them. 'Don't give up hope, Pup.'

'There is no hope,' said Pup. 'Not for a dog like me.'

'What do you mean?' whispered Merle.

'I'm a biter now,' said Pup. 'And I'm sure you know what humans do to biters. They did it to Rex and they'll do it to me too.'

'They can't,' whimpered Merle.

'They can, and they will,' said Pup.

'Make them change that,' insisted Merle. 'Make them see you've changed.'

'I don't want to,' said Pup. 'I don't want to be part of their world any more.' He turned his back on Merle and escaped back into a deep and troubled sleep.

When the Lookers arrived the next day, Pup stayed at the back of his kennel. He watched a woman arrive at Merle's kennel with one of the Aprons.

The woman bent down to put a new collar on Merle. 'Hello again,' she said to Merle. 'I've come to take you home with me.' She looked up at the Apron. 'I've always wanted another collie. My father used to have them on his farm. I don't have the energy for a pup, but I'm sure she and I will have wonderful times.'

Merle got to her feet and followed the woman. She stopped at Pup's kennel and looked in. 'Don't give up, Pup. Someone will come.'

But Pup stayed curled up. He turned his back on the world and closed his eyes. He didn't want to eat or drink. He just waited for the day the Aprons would lead him through the Door of No Return and take him away.

Chapter 36
THE DOG WITH NO NAME

THE NEXT DAY WAS ANOTHER visiting day for the Lookers. Pup tried to block out the sounds of human voices, of children's squeals and laughter. He didn't eat his food, and when one Apron put down some cooked chicken, he growled at her.

Another Apron bent down. 'Poor thing. Reckon he was a fighting dog.'

The first Apron looked up at the notes on the kennel. 'He doesn't have a name.'

'Best not give him one,' said the other. 'It only makes you close to them. Not much chance for this one. No way he can be rehomed.'

The Aprons moved on, and Pup closed his eyes. He felt caged, looked at and trapped. He no longer wanted to run. He just wanted to sleep. To sleep for ever and shut out the world.

There weren't many Lookers today. Rain pattered on the roof, but there were no windows and Pup couldn't see the sky. He tried to remember the days in the Railway Den with Frenchi, feeling the wind and rain on his coat and trotting with Frenchi alongside the river. He remembered playing mad chasing games with Clown in the park and listening to Saffy's stories in the safety of the den. Pup tried to lose himself in dreams, finding sanctuary in sleep.

The Aprons came to take the dogs to the outside runs as the last few visitors trickled in. Soon Pup was the only dog left in a kennel. He became aware of the stillness and the silence. Maybe this was the time the Aprons came to take him away. Maybe this is how it happened. He'd soon be led through the Door of No Return.

Pup curled up, burying his nose deep in his fur. He tried to block out the kennels and tried to think of Frenchi. But his mind kept taking him further back to his boy and the feeling of his boy's arms around him, of his boy curled up next to him in bed, holding his paw in his hand and breathing warm breath into his fur. He lingered on the memory. He had lost his faith in humans, but he still loved his boy. Maybe this was enough, he thought. Maybe it was enough, to know he had been loved. Maybe this was what Saffy had spoken of, the Lupus bond, that couldn't be broken. He tried to remember every small moment with his boy, and he let the memories flood through him. He was so far away in his thoughts, running with his boy through shafts of sunlight, that the bangs and scrapes of doors being opened and shut faded into the background. Somewhere one of the Aprons was shouting and a kennel bolt clanged open.

But Pup was lost deep in the memory of his boy. He could smell him, the delicious scent of football socks and cheese puffs.

'Pup, is that you?'

Pup buried his nose further into his fur, trying not to lose the memory of his boy, trying not to lose the scent of him.

Always trust your nose, Frenchi had said. *It won't let you down.*

'Pup, is that you?'

Pup opened his eyes and sniffed the air. A young man

was crouched in the open doorway looking at him. Pup recognized the young man's eyes and the scent of football socks and cheese puffs.

An Apron tried to pull the young man away. 'Please get away, sir. This is a dangerous dog.'

But the young man knelt forward and reached out a hand to stroke the soft fur on Pup's head. 'Pup, is that you?'

Pup felt his boy's hand on him and felt a rush of recognition and love. It filled his body and soul. He leaped up, his tail wagging so hard that his body swung from side to side. He felt his boy's arms around him and his boy's hot tears soak into his fur.

His boy held him tight. 'Pup, is it really you?'

'It is me,' yelped Pup.

'It's me.

It's me.

It's me.'

Chapter 37
PUP AND HIS BOY

THE APRON SAID IT WAS lucky for Pup that his boy had found him in time. But it wasn't luck that brought Pup and his boy together. It was because his boy had never given up hope of finding him. He had never stopped looking for his dog.

When he did find him, he refused to leave Pup's kennel until the Aprons had signed a form to say they would reassess him and wouldn't put him to sleep. It was obvious to all that Pup had been his dog. But his boy was now a young man and he was old enough to have a dog of his own. He was now an apprentice carpenter and had a room in a house by the canal. His landlady had a soft spot for dogs and let Pup stay too.

And so Pup lived with his boy. Every morning as his boy cycled along the canal towpath to the place where he learned his trade, Pup would run alongside him. He would sleep beneath the workbench, with his nose close to his boy's feet, while sawdust and wood curls fell to the floor. At night he would sleep next to his boy as he had always done as a pup.

One day, not long after his boy had found Pup, he took Pup on a walk up onto the hills above the city. Low cloud drifted over the hilltops. His boy sat down in a hollow sheltered from the wind and broke his sandwich in two to share with Pup. Pup sat next to him, leaning against his boy, looking at the city spread out below them.

'This is my favourite place,' said his boy. He finished his sandwich and put his arm around Pup. 'You were the best thing that ever happened to me. Rory got you off a friend that owed him money. You were a little ball of fluff. He didn't want you, so you became mine. But you didn't like it when I had to go to school.' He grinned. 'You had a good howl. A really good howl. It brought the neighbours and the police around. Mum said we weren't allowed to keep you. She told me Rory had given you to a good home.' He gently stroked Pup's tattered ears. 'But I don't reckon you found a good home, did you?'

Pup licked his hand.

'I never stopped thinking about you,' said his boy. 'I always dreamed you would return, so when I opened the door and saw you that day, I knew you had come back for me. Just me. For the first time in my life, I knew I was loved. Then, when you were taken from me again, I ran away. I ran up here. And I knew that I'd find you. I had to save you, because, when you found me that day, you saved me too.'

Pup leaned into his boy. He looked down at the city, at the grey buildings and the bright patches of green of the parks. It was as if his life had been spread out beneath him. He could see the railway station where Frenchi had taken him to the den that first night. He could see the long brown river curling through the city and the square building of Dogsdoom in the distance. He wondered about Max and Zofia and baby Lena. But now he was here with his boy.

The bond between them had brought them back together.

Pup had found his boy and all was right with the world.

And no one was ever going to take him away again.

Chapter 38
A WOLF-SHAPED NIGHT

THE YEARS PASSED AND THE seasons turned, and both Pup and his boy saw the fresh bright green springs give way to the mellow dry summers and then to golden autumns and cold dark winters. Pup became a little slower, his older legs stiffer and his breath came a little shorter. His muzzle was peppered with grey hairs, and his once dark whiskers were white. And when he could no longer run alongside his boy's bicycle, his boy set out a little earlier each day to walk along the towpath with Pup, giving Pup time to sniff at all the new exciting smells and time to stop and rest. And when Pup could no longer walk all the way to his boy's workplace, his boy bought a trailer to tow behind his bicycle, so that Pup could sit and feel the wind in his fur and stay with his boy.

When his boy finished his apprenticeship, the first piece of woodwork he made was a dog bed, made from oak and lined with a soft fleecy mattress. But Pup only slept in the dog bed in the day. At night he climbed onto the bed with his boy as he had always done when he was a small pup.

But there came a night when Pup could no longer climb up onto the bed with his boy.

His old hips were too stiff and painful. He was tired and weary, and his chest felt heavy. So his boy laid his blankets on the floor so that he could sleep beside Pup and curl up with him. Pup could feel his boy's arm over him, holding his large paw in his warm human hand. He could hear the thump, thump, thump of his boy's heart and feel his warm breath through his fur, lying with him as they had done all those years ago as a pup and young boy. He felt his boy settle into sleep.

The night folded around them, and a cool breeze blew in from the open window. Pup stared out at the sky scattered with stars. The stars seemed to shine even more brightly this night.

A soft wolf-shaped darkness slipped into the room beside Pup. Its fur sparkled with a light of its own making.

'Do you know my name?' asked the dark wolf.

Pup looked up at him. 'I do,' he said. For he knew it was the Great Sky Wolf standing before him.

'I have come to take you with me,' said the wolf.

Pup looked at his boy. 'I don't want to leave him.'

'You will have to,' said the wolf. 'You knew this day would come.'

'But I love him,' said Pup.

'That will never change,' said the wolf. 'Death takes life. But it cannot take love.'

'He is my boy,' said Pup. 'He will always be my boy.'

The Great Sky Wolf smiled. 'And so it always will be. The bond between you can never be broken. You gave your heart to him, and he gave his to you.' The wolf kissed Pup gently on the nose. 'But your wild soul belongs to me.'

Pup licked his boy's warm hand. 'Goodbye, my boy. My wonderful boy. Goodbye.'

His chest rose and fell for one last time.

And Pup followed the Great Wolf, up into the sky.

Epilogue

WHERE THE OCEAN MEETS THE SKY

Pup feels a breeze ruffle through his fur. His legs no longer ache, and his body feels wonderfully free again. There is cool, soft sand beneath his paws. He sits up and sniffs the air, smelling the salt of the ocean. Behind him rise blue green hills and ahead of him a sandy path winds its way up between the dune grasses. The sun is low in the sky and Pup squints into the light. At the top of the dune stands a dog silhouetted against the sky. It has a barrel-shaped body and a short stubby tail that curls over its back. It's wagging that short stubby tail furiously hard.

'Frenchi?' says Pup. 'Is that you?'

The dog trots down towards him. 'Of course it is,' says Frenchi. His breathing is no longer harsh and laboured. He licks Pup on the nose. 'I've been waiting for you. We all have. Come on.'

Pup follows him up the dune where a huge black dog and yellow Labrador sit in the burnished rays of the setting sun.

'Rex! And Saffy!' barks Pup, bounding up to them. 'You're here too.'

'You've taken your time,' says Rex, giving Pup a gentle shove.

Saffy fusses around him, her tail wagging hard. 'Good to see you, Pup.'

'You were right, Saffy,' says Pup. 'My boy found me. He kept faith in me when I had lost faith in man.'

'The Lupus bond is a sacred bond,' says Saffy.

Rex growls softly and turns away from them. 'I still don't believe in that story of the sacred bond. I don't think we need man at all. But I believe in us, in our friendship. I believe in this pack.'

Saffy shakes the sand from her fur and walks up to Rex, licking his face as she might wash a new-born pup. 'Dearest Rex,' she says. 'I don't suppose it really matters what story any of us believe. It's only love that matters in the end.'

'Maybe that's what the story is about after all,' says Frenchi. 'Sirius gave his love and loyalty, without asking anything in return.'

Rex sighs. 'And dogs are so much better at that than

man.' He pads away from them, down the other side of the dune towards the long strip of sand of the beach. 'Come on.'

Pup stands beside Frenchi and looks at the big sweep of the bay and the vast endless sea. The water has been turned gold by the setting sun, and it's impossible to see where the wet sand ends and where the ocean begins.

There are other dogs on the beach too. A boxer and a foxhound run in crazy mad circles chasing each other, and a small scruffy terrier trots through the shallow waves. A blue-eyed collie runs up to Pup, and circles him. 'One more,' she barks. 'One, two, three, four, five, six, seven and me.' She springs around them. 'All here. All here.'

'Merle, you're here too,' says Pup.

'Come on, let's join the others,' says Frenchi. 'Fifi, Reynard and Clown are waiting for us.'

Pup watches Frenchi and the other dogs trot down to the beach. He lifts his nose to the air to smell the salt of the sea.

'Come on,' barks Frenchi.

'Coming,' calls Pup, and he bounds down the dune to join them, where they all jump around him, greeting him, eight tails wagging.

Then they set off, chasing the setting sun, their bodies arching and bending with their long loping strides. They run together on the wet sand where the golden surf foams and unfurls.

They are eight dogs running, with the sun on their backs and wind in their fur. Eight dogs running, where the ocean meets the sky, at the very end of the world.